LONGMAN LITERATURE

The Duchess of Malfi

John Webster

Editor: Trevor Millum

 LONGMAN

Post-1914 Stories from other Cultures

Angelou, Goodison, Senior & Walker **Quartet of Stories** 0 582 28730 8
Nadine Gordimer **July's People** 0 582 06011 7
Ruth Prawer Jhabvala **Heat and Dust** 0 582 25398 5
Alan Paton **Cry, the Beloved Country** 0 582 07787 7
selected by Madhu Bhinda **Stories from Africa** 0 582 25393 4
Stories from Asia 0 582 03922 3
selected by B Naidoo, C Donovan, A Hicks **Global Tales** 0 582 28929 7

Post-1914 Non-Fiction

selected by Geoff Barton **Genres** 0 582 25391 8
selected by Celeste Flower **Diaries and Letters** 0 582 25384 5
selected by Peter Griffiths **Introducing Media** 0 582 28932 7
selected by Linda Marsh **Travel Writing** 0 582 25386 1
Autobiographies 0 582 08837 2

The Diary of Anne Frank 0 582 01736 X

Pre-1914 Fiction

Jane Austen **Pride and Prejudice** 0 582 07720 6
Charlotte Brontë **Jane Eyre** 0 582 07719 2
Emily Brontë **Wuthering Heights** 0 582 07782 6
Charles Dickens **Great Expectations** 0 582 07783 4
Oliver Twist 0 582 28729 4
A Christmas Carol 0 582 23664 9
George Eliot **Silas Marner** 0 582 23662 2
Thomas Hardy **The Mayor of Casterbridge** 0 582 22586 8
Far from the Madding Crowd 0 582 07788 5

Pre-1914 Collections

Thomas Hardy **Wessex Tales** 0 582 25405 1
selected by Geoff Barton **Two Centuries** 0 582 25390 X
Stories Old and New 0 582 28931 9
selected by Jane Christopher **War Stories** 0 582 28927 0
selected by Susie Campbell **Characters from Pre-20th Century Novels** 0 582 25388 8
selected by Celeste Flower **Diaries and Letters** 0 582 25384 5
selected by Linda Marsh **Highlights from 19th-Century Novels** 0 582 25385 3
Landmarks 0 582 25389 6
Travel Writing 0 582 25386 1
selected by Tony Parkinson **Nineteenth-Century Short Stories of Passion and Mystery**
0 582 33807 7

Pre-1914 Poetry

edited by Adrian Tissier **Poems from Other Centuries** 0 582 22585 X

Pre-1914 Plays

Oliver Goldsmith **She Stoops to Conquer** 0 582 25397 7
Henrik Ibsen **Three Plays** 0 582 24948 1
Christopher Marlowe **Doctor Faustus** 0 582 25409 4
selected by Linda Marsh **Starting Shakespeare** 0 582 28930 0
Bernard Shaw **The Devil's Disciple** 0 582 25410 8
Arms and the Man 0 582 07785 0
John Webster **The Duchess of Malfi** 0 582 28731 6
Oscar Wilde **The Importance of Being Earnest** 0 582 07784 2

Contents

CONTENTS

The writer and his world

The facts of John Webster's life are sketchy. There is no evidence of his exact date of birth but most historians put it in 1578 or 1579. We do know that his father was a prosperous coach builder and John went to the prestigious Merchant Taylors' School in London about 1587. He went on to study law at the Middle Temple and there is abundant evidence of his legal training in plays such as **The White Devil, The Devil's Law Case** and **Appius and Virginia**.

Much of Webster's writing was collaborative, beginning with a play called **Caesar's Fall** with three other writers. The next was **Ladey Jane**, another historical drama, in collaboration with, among others, Thomas Dekker with whom he worked again in 1604 on a satirical comedy called **Westward Hoe**. (**Eastward Hoe** was a response by other playwrights and Dekker and Webster replied with **Northward Hoe** in 1605. The idea of sequels to successful dramas was established long before **Jaws II** or **Rocky III**!)

The White Devil

The next published play of which there is a record is **The White Devil**, written in 1612. The first production was not particularly successful, partly due, apparently, to bad weather. It is on this play, together with **The Duchess of Malfi**, that Webster's fame as a dramatist rests.

In **The White Devil**, the Duke of Bracciano's desire for Vittoria leads to Bracciano murdering his own wife and Vittoria's husband. The brother of the murdered Duchess, Francisco, subsequently arranges the killing of Bracciano and Vittoria. He succeeds because he is cleverer, not because he is a more moral person. The central character of the play is Bracciano's secretary, Flamineo, who is also Vittoria's brother. Life at court waiting for the favours of others has corrupted Flamineo. He manages to acquire his sister for his master and his only complaint is his lack of reward.

Vittoria is a sympathetic character in spite of her dubious morality because she challenges society's narrow-mindedness.

> Because she is a woman, Vittoria's freedom of action is very much circum-scribed by a wholly male-oriented society, a society which she must manipu-late as best she can in defence of that independence of mind which characterises her. The only quality which remains to Flamineo and Vittoria in the drawn out scene of their deaths is a sort of personal integrity, a courage in the face of unavoidable suffering.
>
> Anthony Hammond

Neither Vittoria nor Flamineo are heroic characters but they are energetic, even charismatic, personalities for whom it is possible to have some admiration and who certainly retain our interest and curiosity.

Francisco, who carries out the role of revenger, does not experi-ence the moral dilemmas of most revengers. This is a play about people who have lost their moral foundations and are left with no guiding principles except their desires.

The Duchess of Malfi shows a number of similarities to **The White Devil** as will become apparent in the 'Introduction' on page xii. Written in 1613 or 1614, the play was performed by the prestigious King's Men. The great actor Richard Burbage played Ferdinand and it was considered a success.

Of Webster's other work, there is a mysterious 'lost play' called **Guise**, which from the title we assume was also set in Europe. **The Devil's Law Case** which was printed in 1623, has such an incoherent and convoluted plot surrounding the central law case that the play has only been revived once in the intervening years. Webster worked collaboratively again on plays such as **Appius and Virginia** and **A Cure for a Cuckold** but none of these works is of any particular merit. The dramatist is thought to have died in the 1630s.

There are large gaps in our knowledge of Webster and his writing and for all practical purposes **The White Devil** and **The Duchess of Malfi** are the only works of his which have both been performed and continue to be studied in the twentieth century.

The two plays were performed little in the eighteenth century but in the nineteenth Webster's reputation began to grow. In 1808, Charles Lamb quoted extracts from the plays in **Specimens of the English Dramatic Poets**, stressing Webster as a master of the emotions of fear and horror. At the other end of the century, the poet Swinburne rated Webster as second only to Shakespeare.

The Renaissance court

The world of the Italian Renaissance court exercised a fascination over English writers and audiences. There was an admiration for its glamour and worldly success mixed with a disdain for its decadence. The vividness of court life with its moral anarchy masked by princely refinement and ceremony provided ideal dramatic material. Those who wished to make political points closer to home would also choose the Italian setting because writing about the English court was forbidden.

There was also the question of religion. For the majority of English audiences, the Catholicism of the Spanish, Italians and French was not merely a different religion, it was an instrument of wickedness as well as representing a threat to the survival of the Protestant kingdom. Memories of the Armada would be relatively fresh and Catholic plots (real or imagined) were always in the air. The Cardinal in **The Duchess of Malfi**, though a man of God, would be readily accepted as corrupt, as would Ferdinand's representation of the corrupt prince.

Although it was the world of the Italian Renaissance court which caught the imagination of Webster and other writers, the court of Elizabeth and of James I, with its backstabbing, corruption, jealousy and affairs, was not so different from the intrigue of continental courts to which many Englishmen thought themselves superior. For example, Frances Howard, Countess of Somerset, brought a suit of nullity (to annul her marriage) against her husband the Earl of Essex in order to marry Robert Carr, the Earl of Somerset – one of King James's favourites. The writer, Thomas Overbury, was Carr's friend (and known to John Webster) but he opposed the marriage. King James had Overbury imprisoned in the Tower of London, allegedly for refusing to accept a diplomatic appointment. Overbury was poisoned in 1613 by agents of Frances Howard but the story leaked out and the scandal led to the fall from favour of the entire Howard family.

The recurring themes of Jacobean drama, such as lust and moral corruption, are in marked contrast to Shakespeare's wide ranging and often political themes with their Roman and English settings. It is often maintained that drama of this time began a period of decline from which it took many decades to recover – and Webster's plays are sometimes cited as evidence of decadence. In *A Critical History of English Literature*, the critic David Daiches remarks:

> Webster's art ... is decadent, if by decadent we mean the desperate search for effect indulged in by those who work in a literary tradition after it has been fully exploited by a consummate genius.

Certainly Jacobean drama seems to indulge in the melodramatic, to show a desperate striving for effect, to try to pile horror upon horror – often in the manner of a badly made twentieth-century horror film. Subtlety and delicacy were not characteristics much demonstrated on stage at this time.

Tragedy

Tragedy usually begins with an act of defiance against established laws or conventions. These might be the laws of men or of the gods. In Greek tragedy it was commonly the latter. Prometheus, for example, steals fire from Zeus and delivers it to Man; Oedipus kills his father and marries his mother (albeit unknown to him). Both Prometheus and Oedipus are punished for their transgressions. The protagonists, always outstanding figures in some way, are to an extent to blame for their fate – through their pride, their defiance or some other flaw in their character. Through their suffering (and the inevitable suffering caused to others in the events which unfold) the tragic hero comes to a state of greater understanding. Most tragedies end, however, with the hero's death.

In Shakespeare's great tragedies we can see these general principles being worked out. Lear's pride and moral blindness; Othello's jealousy; Hamlet's indecision; Macbeth's ambition – all lead to dreadful reversals of fortune, suffering and death, after which the way is left clear for lesser mortals to continue, sadder but hopefully wiser. It is in **Othello** that we meet the character of Iago, one of Shakespeare's greatest villains. Out of jealousy and spite, Iago determines to poison Othello's mind against his young wife Desdemona. There are obvious parallels between the embittered soldier Iago and the malcontent Bosola in **The Duchess of Malfi** – though it is well to remember that such comparisons also bring out strong differences between the plays and their characters. Both Othello and Iago fall from positions of strength and wordly eminence to suffering and death.

Webster's tragedies follow a similar pattern. As you study the play, you will be able to judge how **The Duchess of Malfi** encompasses the principles of tragic drama outlined above.

Jacobean drama developed a sub-genre of tragedy known as revenge tragedy in which a villain's wrongdoing is eventually avenged by a revenger who is also brought down as a result of his actions. *The Duchess of Malfi* would have been seen by audiences of the day as broadly fitting into this category. Plays which would have been clearly recognised as revenge tragedies include Tourner's *Revenger's Tragedy*, Kyd's *Spanish Tragedy* and Middleton's *The Changeling*.

Hamlet is often cited as a classic example of a revenge tragedy, although it is a great deal more than that. Hamlet suspects his uncle, Claudius, of murdering his father; he feels a duty to avenge his father but is too scrupulous to strike down Claudius in cold blood. He does eventually bring about Claudius' death but in the process is himself killed – along with most of the other major characters.

Machiavelli

In 1532 the Italian writer, Machiavelli, published a book called *The Prince*. It was based on the writer's experience in government in a turbulent period of Italian history. *The Prince* was intended as a handbook for rulers and is seen as being realistic to the extent of being cynical and amoral. Machiavelli would recommend a ruler to do evil if he judged that good would be the eventual result: 'The end justifies the means'. While much criticised for a seeming lack of principle, *The Prince* probably reflects political practice better than most other works on the subject.

The idea that deception (as well as much worse crimes) for political ends is fully justified echoes some of the events of our own time and puts characters such as Ferdinand and the Cardinal into perspective. Though not a politician, a mercenary such as Bosola would have had a similar attitude in that he would serve whoever employed and paid him, regardless of principle. We can imagine both Ferdinand and the Cardinal agreeing wholeheartedly with Machiavelli's statement that 'A wise ruler ... cannot and should not keep his word when it would be to his disadvantage.'

Society

As in most periods of history, society in Jacobean times was organ-ised according to a rigid hierarchy. The pinnacle of this hierarchy was the king or queen and their family. Beneath this was the nobility. The remainder, however wealthy, would be thought of as 'commoners' — hence the House of Commons. Even in the twentieth century there have been instances of members of the British Royal Family being unable to marry the person of their choice because that person was a commoner. Although most states are now based on the principle of equality and aristocracies based simply on blood are rare, it is equally rare to find a society where there are not well understood layers of class. Snobbery is a major factor even in societies as supposedly classless as that of the USA.

Hence, while Webster's audience might sympathise with the Duchess of Malfi for wanting to marry a commoner, they would easily understand the strong pressures against doing so and might well expect such a relationship to end unhappily.

In the Italian society portrayed in **The Duchess of Malfi** and **The White Devil**, the political organisation would have differed from that of today in so far as the area now known as Italy was at that time split (as was Germany) into a multitude of small and often warring states. The Pope was also a ruler of a country and had enormous political and military influence as well as religious powers. Malfi would have been a small but significant dukedom and the brothers of the Duchess, who exercised power in their own right elsewhere, would have been very conscious of their status and the honour of the family name.

Introduction

The play's structure

In many ways the plot of **The Duchess of Malfi** is extremely simple. A noble widow secretly marries someone of lesser birth in defiance of her brothers. When they discover the truth they have her murdered. There is no subplot of any significance and no complexities along the way. As a result, the power and interest of the play lie more in how the plot is worked out than in the development of the story.

Given the simplicity of the plot, it is perhaps surprising that much fault has been found with it over the years. The main reason for this is the fact that the Duchess dies in Act 4 and the following Act is therefore something of an anti-climax. In most tragedies, be they Greek or Shakespearian, the main character dies at the end of the play, usually in the final scene. A few valedictory words are said, conclusions drawn and the play brought to a swift close. For example, after the death of Hamlet there are a mere nine speeches remaining; similarly, following the death of King Lear there are only nine brief utterances before the end. This is not so in **The Duchess of Malfi**. There is a full fifth Act of 678 lines to follow.

The problem does not end with the structure of the play. Many have found the language itself in decline after the much praised Act 4. Following the Duchess's 'I'll tell thee a miracle' speech (Act 4, scene 2, lines 24–31), comments L.G. Salingar in **New Pelican Guide to English Literature**, 'The remainder of the action consists of tedious moralising, posturing and blood-and-thunder.'

Other criticisms have centred on the motivation of some of the central characters. In a play, the plot does not drive itself: characters must do things in order for the drama to unfold – and what they do is carried out for a reason, a motive. In **The Duchess of Malfi** the audience's first question is why the Duchess's brothers are so vehement that she should not remarry. They forbid her to remarry, after all, before any question arises of her marrying beneath her. The frenzy of Ferdinand is almost inexplicable, even bearing in mind the customs and expectations of Renaissance Italy.

Various reasons are proposed for the brothers' prohibition: the feeling of the period that widows should not remarry; that to do so showed a lascivious nature; that those of noble blood should not marry commoners, and that by doing so their sister had sullied the family name and the Cardinal's and Ferdinand's honour. There is also a mention, late in the play, that Ferdinand stood to gain by inheritance an 'infinite mass of treasure' if his sister did not remarry. This is never explained – she has a son by her first marriage, after all. Further explanations of Ferdinand's manic fury are based on his supposed incestuous love for her and stage productions often hint strongly at this. If this is the case, Webster is uncharacteristically restrained in making so little direct mention of it.

There are other unresolved problems of plot and motivation which you may encounter as you read or watch the play.

Some critics maintain that 'realism' was not a prime concern of Webster – or indeed of many Jacobean dramatists – and that we should not worry too much about inconsistencies. After all, the great morality and mystery plays of medieval times dispensed with any necessity for realism and produced powerful drama and moving poetry.

However, Webster is writing stories which have a setting in the real world and purport to deal with real human emotions and actions. As such he should be judged in the context of what he sets out to do and it must be said that there *are* serious flaws in plot structure and characterisation. As David Daiches (op. cit.) says, comparing Webster to another dramatist of the period, he is 'a greater poet than Tourneur but he has less control over dramatic structure.'

No one would argue with the fact that **The Duchess of Malfi** has an episodic structure and that there are sudden and sometimes disconcerting jumps in time – most noticeably when we meet the Duchess again at the beginning of Act 3 and discover that sufficient time has passed for her to have given birth to two more children.

The play's admirers point out that structural coherence was not the prime concern of theatre-goers of the period. They desired striking episodes and memorable language. 'Eloquence was the very breath of drama ... more like the score of an opera than the text of a novel' (Scott Kilvert). Act 4 is admired above all others. It

> ... opens onto a wider universe which transcends common experience: action moves on the psychological plane to the frontiers of madness ... Time and place seem to be suspended.
>
> Scott Kilvert, **Writers and their Work: John Webster**

The poet and critic T.S. Eliot made the point that Webster's verse is 'essentially dramatic verse, written for the theatre by a man with a very acute sense of the theatre', though we should bear in mind that this comes from a man who himself wrote several unsuccessful and rarely performed verse dramas.

It is the general consensus, however, that the strength of **The Duchess of Malfi** lies not in plot but in character and language.

Major characters

You will form your own opinions of the characters in **The Duchess of Malfi** but it is probably true to say that none of the major characters can be easily summed up. Some critics maintain that this is because they are complex, truly human creations with all the paradoxes which that involves. Others have found the characters not so much full of interesting paradoxes as riven by contradictions. Of the main characters, the Duchess and Antonio are the most straightforward and exhibit the clearest motives. Bosola and Ferdinand are the most difficult to understand fully, with Delio and the Cardinal falling somewhere in between.

What follows is not a definitive character study but some starting points for you to consider in your own reflections on the play's personalities.

The Duchess

The central character, of course, is the Duchess. She is admired by many as a heroic figure because of the way she stands out against convention. She is seen as a romantic figure because – against the odds – she marries for love. She is seen as a great tragic figure who dies for doing what she believes in and whose stature grows as her suffering increases. She is also seen as a graceful and intelligent heroine who charms Antonio with a mixture of wit and innuendo.

On the other hand, her heroic stature is diminished by the fact that she does not stand out publicly against convention but marries in secret and tries to keep her marriage – and her three children – from the knowledge of the world. She is not a great figurehead, rallying others to her or defending the rights of others to do the same – hers is a very private, some would say selfish, rebellion.

Nonetheless, she is a romantic figure, perhaps all the more so because of the futility and desperation inherent in her actions. She marries for love – but as a result her husband and two of her children die.

How far the Duchess is a tragic heroine in the traditional sense is open to debate. Would her tragic flaw be impulsiveness or lust? Would she otherwise be great – and does her fall affect the fortunes of states or nations? Compared to most of the great dramatic tragedies, that of the Duchess seems to be more parochial, even domestic.

We can see the graceful and intelligent heroine throughout the first three Acts. She has a quick mind and an eloquent tongue.

> The misery of us, that are born great,
> We are forc'd to woo, because none dare woo us:
> And as a tyrant doubles with his words,
> And fearfully equivocates: so we
> Are forc'd to express our violent passions
> In riddles, and in dreams, and leave the path
> Of simple virtue, which was never made
> To seem the thing it is not.

Act 1, scene 2, lines 360–7

She is not intelligent enough, though, to see through Bosola's duplicity or to have made plans in the event of discovery. The existence of a husband and three children could not be expected to go undetected for ever and her belief that her brothers will come round to accepting it in time seems based more on wishful thinking than insight into their characters.

In spite of the fact that she is the heroine and that she is the prime mover throughout the relationship with Antonio, she is rarely proactive. It is others who act and she who responds to their actions. She is capable of intrigue and deceit, we know, but her actions when compared to those of Bosola and her brothers seem naïve, almost childlike. She does not plot *against* anyone, she merely wishes to hide her actions. Once she has achieved her domestic goal, she has no further aims.

As such, her punishment by the brothers seems all the more inhuman and out of proportion. Were she a figure of greater stature: more heroic, more tragic, the forces unleashed against her would seem more in keeping. As it is, Ferdinand's pitiless torture is merely the action of a madman – and, as a result, the play seems to have more in common with the psychological drama of the twentieth century than with the tragic drama of preceding centuries.

The Duchess's attitude to death is stoical and accepting. In direct contrast to the totally unaccepting and very human death of her maidservant Cariola, she remains dignified and almost impersonal: 'For know, whether I am doom'd to live, or die, I can do both like a prince' (Act 3, scene 2, lines 70–1).

Bosola

There is a certain type of villain of which Bosola is but one example. There is another example in Webster's other great play: Flamineo in **The White Devil**. In Shakespeare we can cite Edmund in **King Lear**, Don John in **Much Ado About Nothing** and Iago in **Othello**. All of these men are bitter because of some real or imagined slight, a resentment at a lack of success or lack of promotion and an envy of those who are more fortunate. Not only do they plot against the hero or heroine, they also provide a cynical commentary on the action.

Bosola is intelligent, brave and patient. He has served the Cardinal as a hired murderer in the past (gaining a prison sentence as a result, it seems) and feels that his service has gone unappreciated. His resentment, logically, should be directed at the Cardinal but is redirected against the Duchess. Perhaps this explains some of the discrepancies in his words and actions; the changes in his attitude towards the Duchess and to Ferdinand, for instance, to whom his relationship can only be described as ambivalent.

Bosola sees humanity as inherently violent, deceitful and bestial – and there is also an underlying sense of disgust in his attitude to it:

> Though we are eaten up of lice, and worms,
> And though continually we bear about us
> A rotten and dead body, we delight
> To hide it in rich tissue: ...

Act 2, scene 1, lines 62–5

In spite of this – or perhaps because of it – Bosola is an apt commentator on what goes on around him: observing and philosophising in his cynical and satirical manner – and deflating any pretensions whether in the Duchess or in Ferdinand: '... you/ Are your own chronicle too much: and grossly/ Flatter yourself' (Act 3, scene 1, lines 87–9). His cynical self-seeking view of the world is challenged by the Duchess's refusal to break down completely and he is forced to confront the existence of an alternative way of dealing with the world. Having said that, it is Ferdinand's ingratitude, his unwillingness to reward Bosola for the killings, which appears to be the deciding factor, the turning point, in his attitude!

Bosola, for most of play, is the puppet of Ferdinand and the Cardinal but by the end of the drama his conscience has been rediscovered. It is his revulsion at the deeds he has carried out which provides the dramatic impetus for the fifth Act. The desire for revenge is difficult to square with the cool, calculating and ruthless soldier of fortune displayed earlier in the play. However, believably or not, it is the motivation which brings about his own downfall as well as that of his erstwhile puppet-masters.

Ferdinand

Ferdinand is the third dominant character in the play. His relationship with his sister, with all its signs of only partially repressed incestuous feelings, leads him from jealously and suspicion to obsession through to murderous fury and finally to madness. The lack of an explicit motive for his cruelty towards the Duchess can only be explicable in terms of an unstable personality. His persecution of the Duchess is more reminiscent of Kafka's *The Trial* (in which the hero is prosecuted and eventually executed for a crime which is never stated) than a Renaissance tragedy.

His concern with family honour and both the privileges and the duties of his class is the other characteristic which feeds the manic persecution and eventual destruction of his sister. In his punishment of the Duchess we feel that he is engaged in punishing himself too, his association with his sister being so close. They are, after all, twins – the closest human relationship possible.

However we explain Ferdinand's attitude to his sister, the result is not just her persecution but his madness. In Act 2, his brother, the Cardinal, comments on Ferdinand's reaction to the Duchess's marriage and the birth of the child: 'You fly beyond your reason.' A little earlier Ferdinand rages:

FERDINAND
>   *Rhubarb, oh for rhubarb*
> *To purge this choler; here's the cursed day*
> *To prompt my memory, and here't shall stick*
> *Till of her bleeding heart I make a sponge*
> *To wipe it out.*

CARDINAL
>   *Why do you make yourself*
> *So wild a tempest?*

FERDINAND
>   *Would I could be one,*
> *That I might toss her palace 'bout her ears,*
> *Root up her goodly forests, blast her meads,*
> *And lay her general territory as waste,*
> *As she hath done her honour's.*

Act 2, scene 5, lines 12–21

A personality which begins obsessive and unbalanced descends rapidly to complete insanity – to the extent of showing all the symptoms of lycanthropy: believing oneself to be a wolf. In Ferdinand, Bosola's bestial view of human nature becomes reality.

We should not forget that Ferdinand's evil-doing is not restricted to his relationship with the Duchess. He is known to be a corrupt judge to whom the law is not the means of bringing justice to his people; on the contrary, to him the law is like 'a foul black cobweb to a spider'. Ferdinand is the opposite of the judicious ruler praised by Antonio in the first minutes of the play; he is the poison at the fountain head causing 'death and disease through the whole land' to spread.

The Cardinal

The Cardinal shares Ferdinand's opposition to the Duchess's marriage but remains calm and distant; he is never on stage with his sister alone. His aloof demeanour is in stark contrast to Ferdinand's excesses. He is concerned with family honour and outward appearance rather than with any considerations of morality.

Delio remarks on the Cardinal's reputation. 'They say he's a brave fellow, will play his five thousand crowns at tennis, dance, court ladies, and one that hath fought single combats' (Act 1, scene 2, lines 77–80). However, even these positive aspects – dancing, gambling, womanising and fighting – are odd characteristics to praise in a representative of the Church! Even so, Antonio disagrees – 'some such flashes superficially hang on him, for form: but observe his inward character: he is a melancholy churchman' (Act 1, scene 2, lines 81–3). He is known to be more of a politician than a man of God, getting his way through bribery and corruption. We also shortly discover that he has a mistress, Julia, who is the wife of one of the courtiers, Castruchio.

The Cardinal is more cold-blooded even than Bosola. He gets rid of Julia without any compunction or regret. He is never disturbed by events and never reveals strong emotion or thought. In this respect he is the complete opposite of his brother – and less interesting as a result.

Antonio

The other major character is Antonio but it is significant that he is a long way from being the hero of the play. His role is too subservient to that of the Duchess and his actions are too obviously the desperate reactions of a man out of his depth for him to fulfil that role. Antonio is a well-meaning and honest commoner who marries a noble lady and as a result becomes enmeshed in a world over which he has no control and can exercise little influence. As a result, he gains our sympathy rather than our admiration. His has been a life in the service of others and when they are gone his life has little purpose. 'I would not now/ Wish my wounds balm'd, nor heal'd: for I have no use/ To put my life to' (Act 5, scene 4, lines 61–3).

The language of the play

The effect of the language in a work of literature is of course best appreciated in reading or listening to it as a whole. The cumulative effect of references and images cannot be appreciated by making lists. The power of speeches such as that of the Duchess's

> *What would it pleasure me, to have my throat cut*
> *With diamonds? or to be smothered*
> *With cassia? or to be shot to death, with pearls?*

> Act 4, scene 2, lines 219–21

can only be fully comprehended in context. However, it may help that appreciation if some of the characteristics of Webster's writing can be highlighted in advance.

The writing is thick with imagery, including some striking metaphors, many of them negative: images of death, disease, futility and pain. Here Ferdinand speaks:

> *Apply desperate physic,*
> *We must not now use balsamum, but fire,*
> *The smarting cupping-glass, for that's the mean*
> *To purge infected blood, such blood as hers.*

> Act 2, scene 5, lines 23–6

and here the Duchess:

> *Persuade a wretch that's broke upon the wheel*
> *To have all his bones new set: entreat him live,*
> *To be executed again. Who must dispatch me?*
> *I account this world a tedious theatre,*

> *For I do play a part in't 'gainst my will.*
>
> Act 4, scene 1, lines 80–4

Bosola's last speech includes the lines:

> *We are only like dead walls, or vaulted graves*
> *That, ruin'd, yields no echo.*
>
> Act 5, scene 5, lines 96–7

Even the animal imagery which is frequently used tends to refer to the less attractive, such as 'crows, pies and caterpillar', the ulcerous wolf, lice, worms ... the list is lengthy.

Many of Webster's most successful images are in the form of thumbnail sketches of characters or of humanity in general. As Delio says of Ferdinand:

> *Then the law to him*
> *Is like a foul black cobweb to a spider,*
> *He makes it his dwelling, and a prison*
> *To entangle those shall feed him.*
>
> Act 1, scene 2, lines 102–105

Elsewhere, language is used to emphasise underlying corruption which is masked by a fair outward appearance, as in the following:

> *Thou dost blanch mischief;*
> *Wouldst make it white. See, see; like to calm weather*
> *At sea before a tempest, false hearts speak fair*
> *To those they intend most mischief*
>
> Act 3, scene 5, lines 23–26

Most memorably, this is evident in Bosola's response to the Duchess's question 'Who am I?'

> *Thou art a box of worm seed, at best, but a salvatory of green mummy: what's this flesh? a little cruded milk, fantastical puff-paste: our bodies are weaker than those paper prisons boys use to keep flies in: more contemptible; since ours is to preserve earthworms ...*
>
> Act 4, scene 2, lines 128–33

Alongside these unpleasant and often violent images, we find helpful maxims expressing truths about life (such as we might say 'One good turn deserves another' or 'Marry in haste, repent at leisure'). This characteristic of Webster is common in much other writing of the period. These moral sayings, often found at the end of a scene, are called *sententiae* and are printed in italics. They are intended to focus attention on a general principle which the specific action of the play has demonstrated. For example, at the end of Act 3, scene 1:

> *That friend a great man's ruin strongly checks,*
> *Who rails into his belief all his defects.*

They perform a similar function to the Chorus in Greek drama which interrupted the flow of the action, commented upon it and suggested the conclusions the audience should draw. In **The Duchess of Malfi**, the majority are platitudes and seem to be included rather as mottos are in crackers – for the sake of tradition rather than for their intrinsic worth. It is important to give attention not just to the meaning of words but also to their rhythm. This is the case with all literature but is especially significant with words which are intended to be spoken, i.e. drama. The majority of **The Duchess of Malfi** is written in blank verse – that is, unrhymed lines of roughly ten syllables, each containing five stresses. For example:

> Per<u>suade</u> a <u>wretch</u> that's <u>broke</u> up<u>on</u> the <u>wheel</u>

In places this poetic rhythm changes to simple prose; as in Shakespeare, this is often where 'lower class' characters are speaking or are being spoken to. Notice how Bosola speaks to the Old Lady at the beginning of Act 2, scene 1 and that when he begins 'his meditation', the language returns to blank verse. However, there is no strict rule, as courtiers talking to each other frequently revert to prose (e.g. Bosola and Antonio in the same scene). Certainly at moments of high drama, prose will not be used, though the rhythm may sometimes be broken and disjointed to reflect the strong emotions of the speakers. For example, the exchange between Bosola and the Cardinal from where the Cardinal says 'Thou looks't ghastly ...' (Act 5, scene 5, line 8ff). In contrast, moments of lyricism are represented in smooth flowing verse as in these words of Antonio

> Her days are practis'd in such noble virtue,
> That, sure her nights, nay more, her very sleeps,
> Are more in heaven, than other ladies' shrifts.
> Let all sweet ladies break their flatt'ring glasses,
> And dress themselves in her.

Act 1, scene 2, lines 126–30

The play's themes

Darkness

The play is a dark one, both in the literal sense and in its underlying mood. There are many scenes which occur in darkness or semi-darkness. Darkness is appropriate for the deeds that are done and to hide the manifold deceits and secrets.

There is also a moral darkness enveloping the drama. One critic has this to say about Webster's point of view:

> The world as he sees it is a pit of darkness through which men grope their way with a haunting sense of disaster, and the ordeal to which he submits his characters is not merely the end of life but a struggle against spiritual annihilation by the power of evil: it is noticeable that none of them, however intolerable the blows of fate, seeks refuge in suicide.

Scott Kilvert, **Writers and their Work: John Webster**

Several of the characters refer to the futility of human action in a meaningless universe – something we might associate more with the world of Samuel Beckett, the twentieth-century dramatist, than the Renaissance playwright.

Although the Duchess prepares herself humbly for Heaven there is precious little that is spiritually uplifting about the play; it moves in a pagan world where forgiveness and virtue are rare. There are references to the gods playing with human beings as if they were tennis balls, recalling Gloucester's remark in **King Lear**: 'as flies to small boys, so are we to the gods, they kill us for their sport' – a darkly cynical sentiment. There is also the darkness of the mind which manifests itself in madness. The mockery of the scene with the madmen is intended to push the Duchess over the edge into madness herself. This fails and instead it is Ferdinand who becomes utterly deranged.

Deception and corruption

Darkness lends itself to deception. The play is full of deceit. The Duchess deceives Ferdinand and the Cardinal. The Cardinal and Ferdinand employ Bosola to deceive the Duchess. The Cardinal deceives Bosola and Bosola deceives Antonio and the Duchess.

There are other, lesser, deceptions but it is interesting that the audience is rarely deceived. As a result the audience always knows more than the characters who are acting out the play.

In spite of the fact that her motive is love (though Ferdinand perceives it as lust), the Duchess sets out to deceive from the start – and Ferdinand seems to sense that she intends to do exactly what they expressly forbid: 'Hypocrisy is woven of a fine small thread' (Act 1, scene 2, line 236).

The Cardinal's corruption is made very clear early on. His double-dealing with Bosola establishes his character even before we see him with Castruchio's wife, Julia, and Antonio's description of him (Act 1, scene 2, lines 81ff) leaves us in little doubt of what kind of personality to expect.

Not only is the court seen as corrupt, the corrupt nobles of the court see the world as a foul place. Ferdinand, the cruel torturer of his sister and instigator of her death – and that of her innocent children and maidservant – sees the Duchess as corrupt. From the viewpoint of modern psychological theory, Ferdinand's extraordinary outbursts against his sister are some of the most obvious examples of someone projecting on to others what they dislike or fear in themselves.

Fortune's wheel and revenge

The idea that human fortunes rise and fall was a common one in both Medieval and Renaissance culture. There are certainly a number of reversals of fortune in *The Duchess of Malfi*. Antonio rises rapidly, experiences happiness and is then plunged into misfortune. The Duchess descends by degrees from her pinnacle of social and domestic success, through loss of position, family, freedom and finally, her life. The fall of the other major characters from power (with all the pretence and hypocrisy associated with it), to the reality of discovery and death is the burden of the final two Acts. Significantly, no one has risen from bad fortune to good by the end of the play, adding to its atmosphere of doom and futility.

In the popular genre of revenge tragedy there was usually a Villain and an Avenger, though in *The Duchess of Malfi* one of the villains, Bosola, is also the avenger. The Duchess's brothers see themselves as avenging family honour, discovering 'crime' in a 'villain', as they see it, and avenging it by killing the Duchess; we then have Bosola 'discovering' the crime of the brothers and avenging it by killing them. We might see the wheel of fortune in action here – the avenger rising to the top of his power, carrying out revenge and then falling as a result of his own actions. Interestingly, the most obvious character to seek revenge, namely Antonio, does not even hint at doing so.

There are other themes and concerns in the play, some of which you will notice on a second or third reading or viewing. Always bear in mind that *The Duchess of Malfi* is a drama and the presentation of the words by actors on a stage may have a very different effect from their appearance on a page.

Reading log

The Study programme on page 232 provides many ideas and activities for *after* you have read the play. However, you are likely to give a better response to the text if you make some notes as you read. The people who assess your coursework assignments or examination answers are looking for evidence of a personal response to literature; to do well, this should be supported by some close analysis and reference to detail.

Keeping notes as you read should help you to provide this, as well as to keep track of events in the plot, characters and relationships and the time-scheme of the play. When you are reading, stop every so often and use the following prompt questions and suggestions to note down key points and details.

Plot

- What have been the main developments in the plot? Note down exactly where they occur.
- How has the dramatist 'moved the story on' – for example, by introducing a new character, by a sudden revelation or by a change of setting?
- Is there more than one plot – for example a plot and a sub-plot?
- How do you expect the plot/s to develop? As you read on, consider whether you predicted accurately or whether there have been some surprises.

Characters

- What are your initial impressions of the main character/s? Are these impressions confirmed or altered as you read? How?
- Do any of the main characters change or develop through the stories? How and why?
- How are you responding to individual characters? In particular, are you aware that you are identifying or sympathising with any of them? Are you conscious of ways in which the author is making or encouraging you to do this?

Setting

The setting of a novel or play is the place and time in which the events happen. Sometimes the setting involves a particular community or culture. It can often make an important contribution to the prevailing atmosphere of the work.

- How much detail does the dramatist provide about the setting of the play? How much is this done through production notes and how much through the dialogue?
- As you read, how do you imagine the play would look in performance? Think about the overall design of the production, the set, costumes and lighting.
- Does the setting seem to be just a background against which the action takes place – for example because it is concerned with historical events or with the interrelationship between people and their environment?

Themes

The themes of a work of literature are the *broad* ideas or aspects of experience which it is about. There are some themes – love, death, war, politics, religion, the environment – which writers have explored throughout the centuries.

- What theme or themes seem to be emerging in the play?
- How is the theme developed? For example, do different characters represent different attitudes or beliefs?
- Does it seem that the writer wants to express his attitude to a theme, to raise questions, or just to make the reader reflect on it?

Style

- Is the play written in a naturalistic style – in other words, trying to create the illusion for the audience that it is watching real events? Or does the dramatist use techniques which break or prevent this effect, such as characters speaking directly to the audience in soliloquies or asides, or the use of a chorus?
- Note down any interesting or striking use of language, such as powerful words and images which evoke a sense of atmosphere. Include any recurring or similar images.
- What do you think of the dialogue? Do the 'voices' of the characters sound real and convincing? Make a note of any particular features of the language used in the dialogue, such as dialect, colloquialisms, slang or expletives.
- Think about the functions of the dialogue in different scenes. For example, is it used to show characters and relationships, to provide dramatic tension, for humour, to explore theme? Remember it might well have more than one fucntion.

Your personal response

- How are your feelings about the play developing as you read? What have you enjoyed or admired most (or least) and why?
- Has the play made you think about or influenced your views on its theme/s?

The Duchess of Malfi

THE
TRAGEDY

OF THE DVTCHESSE
Of Malfy.

*As it was Presented priuatly, at the Black-
Friers; and publiquely at the Globe, By the
Kings Maiesties Seruants.*

The perfect and exact Coppy, with diuerse
things Printed, that the length of the Play would
not beare in the Presentment.

VVritten by *John Webster.*

Hora.———*Si quid*———
———*Candidus Imperti si non his vtere mecum.*

LONDON:

Printed by N ICHOLAS O KES, for I OHN
W ATERSON, and are to be sold at the
signe of the Crowne, in *Paules*
Church-yard, *1 6 2 3.*

CHARACTERS

in the play

BOSOLA, *gentleman of the horse*
FERDINAND, *Duke of Calabria*
CARDINAL, *his brother*
ANTONIO, *steward of the Duchess' household*
DELIO, *his friend*
FOROBOSCO
MALATESTE, *a Count*
THE MARQUIS OF PESCARA
SILVIO, *a Lord*
CASTRUCHIO, *an old Lord*
RODERIGO
GRISOLAN } *Lords*
THE DUCHESS
CARIOLA, *her woman*
JULIA, *wife to Castruchio and mistress to the Cardinal*
THE DOCTOR
COURT OFFICERS
The several mad men, including: ASTROLOGER, TAILOR, PRIEST,
DOCTOR
OLD LADY
THREE YOUNG CHILDREN
TWO PILGRIMS
ATTENDANTS, LADIES, EXECUTIONERS

2–3 **you return ... in your habit**   you've come back looking like a very formal Frenchman.

  5 **reduce**   restore.

  7 **Quits first**   first of all he leaves.

  8 **sycophants**   flatterers, hypocritical courtiers.

10 **His Master's ...**   presumably meant sarcastically.

12 **common**   available to all, shared.

14 **head**   source (if the head of the state sets a bad example, the whole land will be infected).

18 **Inform him**   tell him of.

19 **presumption**   cheeky, disrespectful.

23 **gall**   boil, sore.

  railing   complaining.

Act One

Scene one

(*Enter* ANTONIO *and* DELIO)

DELIO   You are welcome to your country, dear Antonio,
    You have been long in France, and you return
    A very formal Frenchman, in your habit.
    How do you like the French court?

ANTONIO   I admire it;
    In seeking to reduce both State and people   5
    To a fix'd order, their judicious King
    Begins at home. Quits first his royal palace
    Of flatt'ring sycophants, of dissolute,
    And infamous persons, which he sweetly terms
    His Master's master-piece, the work of Heaven,   10
    Consid'ring duly, that a Prince's court
    Is like a common fountain, whence should flow
    Pure silver-drops in general. But if't chance
    Some curs'd example poison't near the head,
    Death and diseases through the whole land spread.   15
    And what is't makes this blessed government,
    But a most provident Council, who dare freely
    Inform him, the corruption of the times?
    Though some o'th' court hold it presumption
    To instruct Princes what they ought to do,   20
    It is a noble duty to inform them
    What they ought to foresee. Here comes Bosola

(*Enter* BOSOLA)

    The only court-gall: yet I observe his railing
    Is not for simple love of piety:
    Indeed he rails at those things which he wants,   25
    Would be as lecherous, covetous, or proud,

28 **If he had means ... so**   if he was able to be.

29 **haunt**   follow.

32–3 **only the reward ... of it!**   the only reward for doing something well is doing it.

34 **enforce**   push, recommend.

35 **galleys**   criminals were punished by being forced to work rowing great ships.

40 **dog days**   bad times; from the unhealthy hot period of the year associated with the dog star, Sirius, being dominant (11 Aug–19 Sep).

44 **arrant knaves**   complete villains.

46–8 **Some fellows ... make him worse**   Bosola suggests the Cardinal is worse than the devil.

49 **He hath denied ... suit?**   he has refused you a favour?

51 **standing pools**   stagnant water.

52 **pies**   magpies (all these creatures have negative, repulsive associations).

54 **panders**   men who procure women for others, pimps.

55 **horse-leech**   leeches suck blood and then drop off when full.

   I pray ...   I request you (to leave me).

58 **Tantalus**   a figure in Greek myth punished by having food and water placed just out of reach (hence the word tantalise).

Bloody, or envious, as any man,
If he had means to be so. Here's the Cardinal.

(*Enter* CARDINAL)

BOSOLA   I do haunt you still.

CARDINAL   So.   30

BOSOLA   I have done you better service than to be
slighted thus. Miserable age, where only the reward of
doing well, is the doing of it!

CARDINAL   You enforce your merit too much.

BOSOLA   I fell into the galleys in your service, where, for   35
two years together, I wore two towels instead of a shirt,
with a knot on the shoulder, after the fashion of a Roman mantle. Slighted thus? I will thrive some way:
blackbirds fatten best in hard weather: why not I, in
these dog days?   40

CARDINAL   Would you could become honest, –

BOSOLA   With all your divinity, do but direct me the way
to it. I have known many travel far for it, and yet
return as arrant knaves, as they went forth; because
they carried themselves always along with them. (*Exit*   45
CARDINAL) Are you gone? Some fellows, they say, are
possessed with the devil, but this great fellow were able
to possess the greatest devil, and make him worse.

ANTONIO   He hath denied thee some suit?

BOSOLA   He and his brother are like plum trees, that   50
grow crooked over standing pools, they are rich, and
o'erladen with fruit, but none but crows, pies, and
caterpillars feed on them. Could I be one of their
flatt'ring panders, I would hang on their ears like a
horse-leech, till I were full, and then drop off. I pray   55
leave me. Who would rely upon these miserable
dependences, in expectation to be advanc'd tomorrow?
What creature ever fed worse, than hoping Tantalus;
nor ever died any man more fearfully, than he that
hop'd for a pardon? There are rewards for hawks, and   60

72 **murther** murder.

73 **suborn'd** instigated.

79 **immoderate** excessive.

81–3 **want of action ... wearing** lack of activity creates dissatisfaction and like moths they will destroy whatever is near them.

1 **presence** audience chamber, formal meeting place.

2 **partaker of the natures** tell me about the characters of ...

dogs, when they have done us service; but for a soldier,
that hazards his limbs in a battle, nothing but a kind of
geometry is his last supportation.

DELIO   Geometry?

BOSOLA   Ay, to hang in a fair pair of slings, take his lat-   65
ter swing in the world, upon an honourable pair of
crutches, from hospital to hospital: fare ye well sir.
And yet do not you scorn us, for places in the court are
but like beds in the hospital, where this man's head lies
at that man's foot, and so lower and lower.   70

Exit BOSOLA

DELIO   I knew this fellow seven years in the galleys,
For a notorious murther, and 'twas thought
The Cardinal suborn'd it: he was releas'd
By the French general, Gaston de Foix
When he recover'd Naples.

ANTONIO   'Tis great pity   75
He should be thus neglected, I have heard
He's very valiant. This foul melancholy
Will poison all his goodness, for, I'll tell you,
If too immoderate sleep be truly said
To be an inward rust unto the soul,   80
It then doth follow want of action
Breeds all black malcontents, and their close rearing,
Like moths in cloth, do hurt for want of wearing.

Scene two

(*Enter* CASTRUCHIO, SILVIO, RODERIGO *and* GRISOLAN)

DELIO   The presence 'gins to fill. You promis'd me
To make me the partaker of the natures
Of some of your great courtiers.

11

6 **took the ring** gained the prize (in jousting contests a rider had to catch a ring on the tip of his lance). Rings have a significance in the play.

9–10 **when shall we ... indeed** Ferdinand wants to fight in a real battle rather than in sport.

20 **office** tasks, duties.

30 **tents** bandages (a weak pun).

32 **chirurgeons** surgeons.

gallants brave young follows.

ANTONIO   The Lord Cardinal's
And other strangers', that are now in court?
I shall. Here comes the great Calabrian Duke.   5

(*Enter* FERDINAND)

FERDINAND   Who took the ring oft'nest?
SILVIO   Antonio Bologna, my lord.
FERDINAND   Our sister Duchess' great master of her
household? Give him the jewel: when shall we leave
this sportive action, and fall to action indeed?   10
CASTRUCHIO   Methinks, my lord, you should not desire
to go to war, in person.
FERDINAND   (*aside*) Now, for some gravity: why, my lord?
CASTRUCHIO   It is fitting a soldier arise to be a prince,
but not necessary a prince descend to be a captain!   15
FERDINAND   No?
CASTRUCHIO   No, my lord, he were far better do it by a
deputy.
FERDINAND   Why should he not as well sleep, or eat, by a
deputy? This might take idle, offensive, and base office   20
from him, whereas the other deprives him of honour.
CASTRUCHIO   Believe my experience: that realm is never
long in quiet, where the ruler is a soldier.
FERDINAND   Thou told'st me thy wife could not endure
fighting.   25
CASTRUCHIO   True, my lord.
FERDINAND   And of a jest she broke, of a captain she met
full of wounds: I have forgot it.
CASTRUCHIO   She told him, my lord, he was a pitiful
fellow, to lie, like the children of Ismael, all in tents.   30
FERDINAND   Why, there's a wit were able to undo all the
chirurgeons o' the city, for although gallants should
quarrel, and had drawn their weapons, and were ready
to go to it; yet her persuasions would make them put
up.   35

37 **jennet**   horse.

39 **Pliny**   a Roman writer.

40 **begot**   fathered.

40–1 **ballass'd with quick-silver**   weighed down (from ballast) with mercury. (Though mercury is not particularly light, the impression given by its common name implies speed.)

42 **reels from**   shies away from.

   tilt   the joust (a sexual meaning also as in shying away from sexual encounter).

45 **touchwood**   wood used for starting a fire, kindling. Ferdinand is saying that they should wait for him to laugh before doing so themselves.

51 **fool**   court jester also perhaps a double meaning, 'your foolishness'.

52–3 **He cannot ... faces**   he cannot speak without making odd faces.

59–60 **out of compass**   out of control.

65 **Grecian horse**   Trojan horse.

CASTRUCHIO   That she would, my lord.

FERDINAND   How do you like my Spanish jennet?

RODERIGO   He is all fire.

FERDINAND   I am of Pliny's opinion, I think he was
begot by the wind; he runs as if he were ballass'd   40
with quick-silver.

SILVIO   True, my lord, he reels from the tilt often.

RODERIGO *and* GRISOLAN   Ha, ha, ha!

FERDINAND   Why do you laugh? Methinks you that are
courtiers should be my touchwood, take fire when I   45
give fire; that is, laugh when I laugh, were the subject
never so witty, —

CASTRUCHIO   True, my lord, I myself have heard a very
good jest, and have scorn'd to seem to have so silly a
wit, as to understand it.   50

FERDINAND   But I can laugh at your fool, my lord.

CASTRUCHIO   He cannot speak, you know, but he makes
faces; my lady cannot abide him.

FERDINAND   No?

CASTRUCHIO   Nor endure to be in merry company: for   55
she says too much laughing, and too much company,
fills her too full of the wrinkle.

FERDINAND   I would then have a mathematical instrument made for her face, that she might not laugh out of
compass. I shall shortly visit you at Milan, Lord Silvio.   60

SILVIO   Your Grace shall arrive most welcome.

FERDINAND   You are a good horseman, Antonio; you
have excellent riders in France, what do you think of
good horsemanship?

ANTONIO   Nobly, my lord: as out of the Grecian horse   65
issued many famous princes, so out of brave horsemanship, arise the first sparks of growing resolution,
that raise the mind to noble action.

FERDINAND   You have bespoke it worthily.

76–7 **Now sir ... Cardinal?** Now tell me, as you promised, about the character of the Cardinal.

81–2 **Some such ... for form** he has some outward attractiveness.

83 **The spring ... toads** this image that seemingly clear water is in fact a place which breeds toads, suggests that his looks are deceptive.

86 **Hercules** reference to the labours of Hercules.

87 **intelligencers** spies.

88 **political** scheming.

89 **primitive** traditional.

95–7 **What appears ... fashion** the Duke rarely laughs except to poke fun at things that are good and honest.

99 **bench** i.e. the magistrates' bench, court of justice.

(*Enter* DUCHESS, CARDINAL, CARIOLA *and* JULIA)

SILVIO   Your brother, the Lord Cardinal, and sister   70
  Duchess.
CARDINAL   Are the galleys come about?
GRISOLAN   They are, my lord.
FERDINAND   Here's the Lord Silvio, is come to take his
  leave.   75
DELIO   (*aside to* ANTONIO)   Now sir, your promise: what's
  that Cardinal? I mean his temper? They say he's a
  brave fellow, will play his five thousand crowns at
  tennis, dance, court ladies, and one that hath fought
  single combats.   80
ANTONIO   Some such flashes superficially hang on him,
  for form: but observe his inward character: he is a
  melancholy churchman. The spring in his face is nothing but the engend'ring of toads: where he is jealous
  of any man, he lays worse plots for them, than ever   85
  was impos'd on Hercules: for he strews in his way flatterers, panders, intelligencers, atheists: and a thousand
  such political monsters: he should have been Pope: but
  instead of coming to it by the primitive decency of the
  Church, he did bestow bribes, so largely, and so im-   90
  pudently, as if he would have carried it away without
  Heaven's knowledge. Some good he hath done.
DELIO   You have given too much of him: what's his
  brother?
ANTONIO   The Duke there? a most perverse and turbu-
  lent nature;
  What appears in him mirth, is merely outside,   95
  If he laugh heartily, it is to laugh
  All honesty out of fashion.
DELIO   Twins?
ANTONIO   In quality:
  He speaks with others' tongues, and hears men's suits
  With others' ears: will seem to sleep o'th' bench

17

106 **He nev'r pays ... turns** he only repays (revenges) bad turns (deeds).

109 **oracles** wise or prophetic sayings.

114 **one figure** same mould.

temper character; Antonio is saying that although the Cardinal, Ferdinand and the Duchess are brothers and sisters they have totally different characters.

115 **her discourse ... rapture** her conversation is delightful.

118 **vainglory** boastfulness, showing off.

121 **galliard** brisk dance.

122 **palsy** paralysis.

124 **continence** restraint.

127–8 **her very sleeps ... shrifts** even when she is asleep she is more virtuous than other women at confession.

129 **glasses** mirrors.

130 **dress ... her** use her as their model.

131 **wire-drawer** one who extends or spins out wire (i.e. you exaggerate her good qualities).

Only to entrap offenders in their answers; 100
Dooms men to death by information,
Rewards, by hearsay.

DELIO   Then the law to him
Is like a foul black cobweb to a spider,
He makes it his dwelling, and a prison
To entangle those shall feed him.

ANTONIO   Most true: 105
He nev'r pays debts, unless they be shrewd turns,
And those he will confess, that he doth owe.
Last: for his brother, there, the Cardinal,
They that do flatter him most, say oracles
Hang at his lips: and verily I believe them: 110
For the devil speaks in them.
But for their sister, the right noble Duchess,
You never fix'd your eye on three fair medals,
Cast in one figure, of so different temper.
For her discourse, it is so full of rapture, 115
You only will begin, then to be sorry
When she doth end her speech: and wish, in wonder,
She held it less vainglory to talk much
Than your penance, to hear her: whilst she speaks,
She throws upon a man so sweet a look, 120
That it were able to raise one to a galliard
That lay in a dead palsy; and to dote
On that sweet countenance: but in that look
There speaketh so divine a continence,
As cuts off all lascivious, and vain hope. 125
Her days are practis'd in such noble virtue,
That, sure her nights, nay more, her very sleeps,
Are more in heaven, than other ladies' shrifts.
Let all sweet ladies break their flatt'ring glasses,
And dress themselves in her.

DELIO   Fie Antonio 130
You play the wire-drawer with her commendations.

132 **case**   close.

134 **stains**   throws into shade or eclipse.

137 **suit to you**   request.

141 **provisorship ... horse**   an official position in charge of the Duchess's horses.

145 **leaguer**   army camp.

147 **caroches**   carriages.

148 **entertain**   employ.

149–51 **I would not ... morning**   I do not want to be seen to be involved. To that end I've often rebuffed him as I did this morning when he sought a position with me.

ANTONIO   I'll case the picture up: only thus much:
  All her particular worth grows to this sum:
  She stains the time past: lights the time to come.
CARIOLA   You must attend my lady, in the gallery,   135
  Some half an hour hence.
ANTONIO   I shall.

Exeunt ANTONIO *and* DELIO

FERDINAND   Sister, I have a suit to you.
DUCHESS   To me, sir?
FERDINAND   A gentleman here: Daniel de Bosola:
  One, that was in the galleys.
DUCHESS   Yes, I know him.
FERDINAND   A worthy fellow h'is: pray let me entreat for 140
  The provisorship of your horse.
DUCHESS   Your knowledge of him
  Commends him, and prefers him.
FERDINAND   Call him hither.

Exit ATTENDANT

  We are now upon parting. Good Lord Silvio
  Do us commend to all our noble friends
  At the leaguer.
SILVIO   Sir, I shall.   145
DUCHESS   You are for Milan?
SILVIO   I am.
DUCHESS   Bring the caroches: we'll bring you down to the
  haven.

Exeunt DUCHESS, CARIOLA, SILVIO, CASTRUCHIO, RODERIGO,
GRISOLAN *and* JULIA

CARDINAL   Be sure you entertain that Bosola
  For your intelligence: I would not be seen in't.
  And therefore many times I have slighted him,   150
  When he did court our furtherance: as this morning.
FERDINAND   Antonio, the great master of her household
  Had been far fitter.

158 **oblique character**   sinister characteristic.

159 **physiognomy**   facial characteristics, especially the inference of personality from the face's appearance.

162 **cozens**   deceives.

166–7 **the oftshaking ... at root**   the shaking of a great tree fastens it more securely because it gets rid of parasites (presumably hangers-on like Bosola); the cedar symbolises men of stature.

171 **What follows?**   where's the catch? The allusion is to Jupiter's appearance as a shower of gold to get close to Danäe. He was also well known for hurling thunderbolts.

174 **post**   ahead.

CARDINAL You are deceiv'd in him,
His nature is too honest for such business.
He comes: I'll leave you.

(*Enter* BOSOLA)

BOSOLA I was lur'd to you. 155

Exit CARDINAL

FERDINAND My brother here, the Cardinal, could never
Abide you.
BOSOLA Never since he was in my debt.
FERDINAND May be some oblique character in your face
Made him suspect you?
BOSOLA Doth he study physiognomy?
There's no more credit to be given to th' face, 160
Than to a sick man's urine, which some call
The physician's whore, because she cozens him.
He did suspect me wrongfully.
FERDINAND For that
You must give great men leave to take their times:
Distrust doth cause us seldom be deceiv'd; 165
You see, the oft shaking of the cedar tree
Fastens it more at root.
BOSOLA Yet take heed:
For to suspect a friend unworthily
Instructs him the next way to suspect you,
And prompts him to deceive you.
FERDINAND There's gold.
BOSOLA So: 170
What follows? (Never rain'd such showers as these
Without thunderbolts i'th' tail of them;)
Whose throat must I cut?
FERDINAND Your inclination to shed blood rides post
Before my occasion to use you. I give you that 175
To live i'th' court, here: and observe the Duchess,

23

177 **haviour** behaviour.

179 **affects** favours.

183 **familiars** someone who is very close, especially a spirit accompanying a devil or witch usually in the form of an animal (e.g. the witch's cat).

187 **devils** gold coins.

188 **angels** certain gold coins bore pictures of angels.

195 **bounty** generosity.

199–200 **Thus the devil ... o'er** the devil makes sins seem sweet.

200 **vild** vile.

202 **garb** dress, outward appearance.

To note all the particulars of her haviour:
What suitors do solicit her for marriage
And whom she best affects: she's a young widow,
I would not have her marry again.

BOSOLA   No, sir?   180

FERDINAND   Do not you ask the reason: but be satisfied,
I say I would not.

BOSOLA   It seems you would create me
One of your familiars.

FERDINAND   Familiar? what's that?

BOSOLA   Why, a very quaint invisible devil in flesh:
An intelligencer.

FERDINAND   Such a kind of thriving thing   185
I would wish thee: and ere long, thou mayst arrive
At a higher place by't.

BOSOLA   Take your devils
Which hell calls angels: these curs'd gifts would make
You a corrupter, me an impudent traitor,
And should I take these they'll'd take me to hell.   190

FERDINAND   Sir, I'll take nothing from you that I have
   given.
There is a place that I procur'd for you
This morning, the provisorship o'th' horse,
Have you heard on't?

BOSOLA   No.

FERDINAND   'Tis yours, is't not worth thanks?

BOSOLA   I would have you curse yourself now, that your
   bounty,   195
Which makes men truly noble, e'er should make
Me a villain: oh, that to avoid ingratitude
For the good deed you have done me, I must do
All the ill man can invent. Thus the devil
Candies all sins o'er: and what Heaven terms vild,   200
That names he complemental.

FERDINAND   Be yourself:
Keep your old garb of melancholy: 'twill express

205 **politic dormouse**   scheming, though seemingly quiet and inoffensive.

215 **Sometimes ... doth preach**   the devil is capable of delivering a holy sermon.

216 **we are to part ...**   they are speaking to the Duchess.

221 **Sway your high blood**   influence your noble breeding (and/or passionate nature).

    luxurious   lecherous, lustful.

222–3 **Their livers ... Laban's sheep**   the liver was seen to be the source of strong emotion rather as the heart is today. The story of Jacob and Laban can be found in Genesis 29–30.

You envy those that stand above your reach,
Yet 'strive not to come near 'em. This will gain
Access to private lodgings, where yourself
May, like a politic dormouse, —   205
BOSOLA   As I have seen some,
Feed in a lord's dish, half asleep, not seeming
To listen to any talk: and yet these rogues
Have cut his throat in a dream: what's my place?
The provisorship o'th' horse? say then my corruption   210
Grew out of horse dung. I am your creature.
FERDINAND   Away!
BOSOLA   Let good men, for good deeds, covet good fame,
Since place and riches oft are bribes of shame;
Sometimes the devil doth preach.   215

                                              Exit BOSOLA

(*Enter* CARDINAL, DUCHESS *and* CARIOLA)

CARDINAL   We are to part from you: and your own discretion
Must now be your director.
FERDINAND   You are a widow:
You know already what man is: and therefore
Let not youth, high promotion, eloquence, —
CARDINAL   No, nor anything without the addition,
    Honour,   220
Sway your high blood.
FERDINAND   Marry? they are most luxurious,
Will wed twice.
CARDINAL   O fie!
FERDINAND   Their livers are more spotted
Than Laban's sheep.
DUCHESS   Diamonds are of most value
They say, that have pass'd through most jewellers'
    hands.
FERDINAND   Whores, by that rule, are precious.

27

227 **motion**   intention.

230 **rank**   corrupt.

231 **honey-dew**   sticky substance covering plant stems; by implication
something sweet which both traps and stains or poisons.

233 **whose faces ... hearts**   who disguise inner feelings.

235 **give the devil suck**   reference to the belief that witches suckled evil
spirits/familiars.

237 **Vulcan's engine**   the trap made by Vulcan to ensnare his wife (Venus)
and her lover (Mars) which was a net made of the finest mesh.

242 **irregular crab**   in fact crabs seem to walk sideways.

246 **executed**   formally carried out; also a reference to death.

DUCHESS   Will you hear me? 225
  I'll never marry—
CARDINAL   So most widows say:
  But commonly that motion lasts no longer
  Than the turning of an hourglass; the funeral sermon
  And it, end both together.
FERDINAND   Now hear me;
  You live in a rank pasture; here, i'th' court,   230
  There is a kind of honey-dew that's deadly:
  'Twill poison your fame; look to't; be not cunning:
  For they whose faces do belie their hearts
  Are witches, ere they arrive at twenty years,
  Ay: and give the devil suck.
DUCHESS   This is terrible good counsel. 235
FERDINAND   Hypocrisy is woven of a fine small thread,
  Subtler than Vulcan's engine: yet, believe't,
  Your darkest actions: nay, your privat'st thoughts,
  Will come to light.
CARDINAL   You may flatter yourself,
  And take your own choice: privately be married   240
  Under the eaves of night—
FERDINAND   Think't the best voyage
  That e'er you made; like the irregular crab,
  Which, though't goes backward, thinks that it goes
    right,
  Because it goes its own way: but observe:
  Such weddings may more properly be said   245
  To be executed, than celebrated.
CARDINAL   The marriage night
  Is the entrance into some prison.
FERDINAND   And those joys,
  Those lustful pleasures, are like heavy sleeps
  Which do forerun man's mischief.
CARDINAL   Fare you well.
  Wisdom begins at the end: remember it.   250

Exit CARDINAL

251 **studied** rehearsed.

252 **roundly** smoothly.

253 **poniard** dagger.

255 **chargeable revels** expensive hospitality, entertaining.

256 **visor ... mask** used for dressing up, for disguises at dances – such disguises could be used to hide love affairs.

258 **lamprey** fish supposed to lack bones, here used for crude sexual innuendo.

261 **neat** handsome.

265 **make ... foot-steps** she would use them as steps up towards her goal.

269 **assay** try.

271 **winked** chose rapidly, without thinking (or without regard to consequences).

272 **secrecy** ability to keep secrets.

277 **ingenious and hearty** naive and heartfelt.

DUCHESS   I think this speech between you both was studied,
It came so roundly off.

FERDINAND   You are my sister,
This was my father's poniard: do you see,
I'll'd be loath to see't look rusty, 'cause 'twas his.
I would have you to give o'er these chargeable revels;   255
A visor and a mask are whispering-rooms
That were nev'r built for goodness: fare ye well:
And women like that part, which, like the lamprey,
Hath nev'r a bone in't.

DUCHESS   Fie sir!

FERDINAND   Nay,
I mean the tongue: variety of courtship;   260
What cannot a neat knave with a smooth tale
Make a woman believe? Farewell, lusty widow.

Exit FERDINAND

DUCHESS Shall this move me? If all my royal kindred
Lay in my way unto this marriage,
I'll'd make them my low foot-steps. And even now,   265
Even in this hate, (as men in some great battles
By apprehending danger, have achiev'd
Almost impossible actions: I have heard soldiers say
   so,)
So I, through frights and threat'nings, will assay
This dangerous venture. Let old wives report   270
I winked, and chose a husband. Cariola,
To thy known secrecy I have given up
More than my life, my fame.

CARIOLA   Both shall be safe:
For I'll conceal this secret from the world
As warily as those that trade in poison,   275
Keep poison from their children.

DUCHESS   Thy protestation
Is ingenious and hearty: I believe it.
Is Antonio come?

279 *arras*   wall hanging.

282 *clew*   not clue, but thread to guide someone through a maze.

287 *triumphs*   entertainment.

288 *husbands*   husband can mean spouse but also has a more formal sense of being in charge of a household, a steward.

292 *tane*   taken.

CARIOLA He attends you.

DUCHESS Good dear soul,
  Leave me: but place thyself behind the arras,
  Where thou mayst overhear us: wish me good speed   280
  For I am going into a wilderness,
  Where I shall find nor path, nor friendly clew
  To be my guide.

(CARIOLA *goes behind the arras. Enter* ANTONIO.)

  I sent for you. Sit down:
  Take pen and ink, and write. Are you ready?

ANTONIO Yes.

DUCHESS What did I say?

ANTONIO That I should write somewhat.   285

DUCHESS Oh, I remember:
  After these triumphs and this large expense
  It's fit, like thrifty husbands, we inquire
  What's laid up for tomorrow.

ANTONIO So please your beauteous excellence.

DUCHESS Beauteous?   290
  Indeed I thank you: I look young for your sake.
  You have tane my cares upon you.

ANTONIO I'll fetch your Grace
  The particulars of your revenue and expense.

DUCHESS Oh, you are an upright treasurer: but you mis-
      took,
  For when I said I meant to make inquiry   295
  What's laid up for tomorrow: I did mean
  What's laid up yonder for me.

ANTONIO Where?

DUCHESS In heaven.
  I am making my will, as 'tis fit princes should
  In perfect memory, and I pray sir, tell me
  Were not one better make it smiling, thus?   300
  Than in deep groans, and terrible ghastly looks,

302 **procur'd** caused.

305 **overseer** executor, one who looks after the carrying out of a will.

311 **winding sheet** shroud; cloth in which one is buried.

  In a couple in two sheets, i.e. bedsheets.

316–7 **It locally ... in't** marriage constitutes either heaven or hell – one or the other and nothing in between.

317 **affect it** think of it.

318 **banishment** his recent absence in France.

323 **wanton** rascal, affectionate term for a child.

327 **sovereign** effective.

As if the gifts we parted with, procur'd
That violent distraction?
ANTONIO   Oh, much better.
DUCHESS If I had a husband now, this care were quit:
But I intend to make you overseer;   305
What good deed shall we first remember? Say.
ANTONIO Begin with that first good deed, begin i'th' world,
After man's creation, the sacrament of marriage.
I'ld have you first provide for a good husband,
Give him all.
DUCHESS   All?
ANTONIO   Yes, your excellent self.   310
DUCHESS In a winding sheet?
ANTONIO   In a couple.
DUCHESS St. Winifred! that were a strange will.
ANTONIO   'Twere strange
If there were no will in you to marry again.
DUCHESS What do you think of marriage?
ANTONIO I take't, as those that deny purgatory,   315
It locally contains or heaven, or hell;
There's no third place in't.
DUCHESS   How do you affect it?
ANTONIO My banishment, feeding my melancholy,
Would often reason thus:-
DUCHESS   Pray let's hear it.
ANTONIO Say a man never marry, nor have children,   320
What takes that from him? only the bare name
Of being a father, or the weak delight
To see the little wanton ride a-cock-horse
Upon a painted stick, or hear him chatter
Like a taught starling.
DUCHESS   Fie, fie, what's all this?   325
One of your eyes is bloodshot, use my ring to't,
They say 'tis very sovereign: 'twas my wedding ring,
And I did vow never to part with it,
But to my second husband.

332–3 *a saucy ... circle* Antonio's thoughts about the possibilities of marriage to the Duchess; she also in her way is being saucy and ambitious.

336 *roof* head.

338 *Without* unless.

340–4 *Ambition, Madam ... all cure* Antonio sees ambition as the madness of the great – not the kind of madness which is kept under lock and chains but which, though it exists in fair surroundings, is nevertheless equally lunatic.

345–6 *Conceive not ... tend* don't think I'm so stupid that I don't guess where your favours are leading.

351–9 *You were ill ... wages of her* the Duchess makes much of Antonio's modesty and contrasts it with the traders who try to sell their wares in poor lighting to hide their faults. Antonio replies that he has always been virtuous without expecting reward.

ANTONIO   You have parted with it now.
DUCHESS   Yes, to help your eyesight.   330
ANTONIO   You have made me stark blind.
DUCHESS   How?
ANTONIO   There is a saucy and ambitious devil
   Is dancing in this circle.
DUCHESS   Remove him.
ANTONIO   How?
DUCHESS   There needs small conjuration, when your finger
   May do it: thus, is it fit?

(*She puts the ring on his finger.*) *He kneels.*

ANTONIO   What said you?
DUCHESS   Sir?   335
   This goodly roof of yours, is too low built,
   I cannot stand upright in't, nor discourse,
   Without I raise it higher: raise yourself,
   Or if you please, my hand to help you: so. (*Raises him*)
ANTONIO   Ambition, Madam, is a great man's madness,   340
   That is not kept in chains, and close-pent rooms,
   But in fair lightsome lodgings, and is girt
   With the wild noise of prattling visitants,
   Which makes it lunatic, beyond all cure.
   Conceive not, I am so stupid, but I aim   345
   Whereto your favours tend. But he's a fool
   That, being a-cold, would thrust his hands i'th' fire
   To warm them.
DUCHESS   So, now the ground's broke,
   You may discover what a wealthy mine
   I make you lord of.
ANTONIO   O my unworthiness!   350
DUCHESS   You were ill to sell yourself;
   This dark'ning of your worth is not like that
   Which tradesmen use i'th' city; their false lights
   Are to rid bad wares off: and I must tell you
   If you will know where breathes a complete man,   355

37

362 **doubles** is ambiguous – same meaning as equivocates in line 363.

373 **alabaster** a stone often used in the carving of effigies and monuments to the dead.

379 **sanctuary** protection.

383 **Quietus est** (Latin) 'It is finished' as used in accounts but with undertones of death.

384 **thus** presumably Antonio is hesitant in his reaction to her kiss.

(I speak it without flattery), turn your eyes,
And progress through yourself.
ANTONIO   Were there nor heaven, nor hell,
   I should be honest: I have long serv'd virtue,
   And nev'r tane wages of her.
DUCHESS   Now she pays it.
   The misery of us, that are born great,   360
   We are forc'd to woo, because none dare woo us:
   And as a tyrant doubles with his words,
   And fearfully equivocates: so we
   Are forc'd to express our violent passions
   In riddles, and in dreams, and leave the path   365
   Of simple virtue, which was never made
   To seem the thing it is not. Go, go brag
   You have left me heartless, mine is in your bosom,
   I hope 'twill multiply love there. You do tremble:
   Make not your heart so dead a piece of flesh   370
   To fear, more than to love me. Sir, be confident,
   What is't distracts you? This is flesh, and blood, sir,
   'Tis not the figure cut in alabaster
   Kneels at my husband's tomb. Awake, awake, man,
   I do here put off all vain ceremony,   375
   And only do appear to you, a young widow
   That claims you for her husband, and like a widow,
   I use but half a blush in't.
ANTONIO   Truth speak for me,
   I will remain the constant sanctuary
   Of your good name.
DUCHESS   I thank you, gentle love,   380
   And 'cause you shall not come to me in debt,
   Being now my steward, here upon your lips
   I sign your *Quietus est*. This you should have begg'd
     now:
   I have seen children oft eat sweetmeats thus,
   As fearful to devour them too soon.   385
ANTONIO   But for your brothers?

387 **circumference**   their arms – or perhaps the confines of the room?

390 **Scatter the tempest**   calm their anger.

395 **Per verba de presenti**   (Latin) 'By words about the present' – the simple statement of their vows before a witness would be a legally binding marriage though disapproved of by the church.

396 **Gordian**   a reference to the Gordian knot of legend which could not be untied, only cut.

399 **still**   always.

   Quick'ning   coming alive.

400 **music**   the music of the spheres was a Renaissance idea which held that perfect music was created by the movement of the planets in their appointed orbits.

404 **force**   enforce.

407 **faster**   more securely, as in held fast.

410 **blind**   Fortune was blind.

   conceit   meaning.

DUCHESS   Do not think of them:
　All discord, without this circumference,
　Is only to be pitied, and not fear'd.
　Yet, should they know it, time will easily
　Scatter the tempest.
ANTONIO   These words should be mine,   390
　And all the parts you have spoke, if some part of it
　Would not have savour'd flattery.
DUCHESS   Kneel.

(*Enter* CARIOLA)

ANTONIO   Ha?
DUCHESS   Be not amaz'd, this woman's of my counsel.
　I have heard lawyers say, a contract in a chamber,
　Per verba de presenti, is absolute marriage.   395
　Bless, Heaven, this sacred Gordian, which let violence
　Never untwine.
ANTONIO   And may our sweet affections, like the spheres,
　Be still in motion.
DUCHESS   Quick'ning, and make
　The like soft music.   400
ANTONIO   That we may imitate the loving palms,
　Best emblem of a peaceful marriage,
　That nev'r bore fruit divided.
DUCHESS   What can the Church force more?
ANTONIO· That Fortune may not know an accident   405
　Either of joy or sorrow, to divide
　Our fixed wishes.
DUCHESS   How can the Church build faster?
　We now are man and wife, and 'tis the Church
　That must but echo this. Maid, stand apart,
　I now am blind.
ANTONIO   What's your conceit in this?   410
DUCHESS   I would have you lead your fortune by the
　　hand,
　Unto your marriage bed:

414–5 *plot ... kindred* plan how to pacify my ill-tempered relations.
 418 *shroud* veil, hide.

(You speak in me this, for we now are one)
We'll only lie, and talk together, and plot
T'appease my humorous kindred; and if you please,   415
Like the old tale, in *Alexander and Lodowick*,
Lay a naked sword between us, keep us chaste.
Oh, let me shroud my blushes in your bosom,
Since 'tis the treasury of all my secrets.

CARIOLA   Whether the spirit of greatness, or of woman   420
Reign most in her, I know not, but it shows
A fearful madness: I owe her much of pity.

Exeunt

1 *fain*   desire to.

3 *main*   central purpose.

5 *nightcap*   refers to the head covering worn by lawyers (cf. barristers' wigs).

   expresses   pushes out.

7 *band*   decorative neck-band worn by lawyers.

10 *president*   judge, magistrate.

15 *a nights*   at night.

18 *roaring boys*   young bloods, riotous young men.

22–3 *give out ... a-dying*   let it be known that you're dying.

24 *prime nightcaps*   eminent lawyers (see also note to line 5 above).

25 *painting*   putting on make-up.

27 *scurvy face physic*   medicine for a diseased face.

Act Two

Scene one

(*Enter* BOSOLA *and* CASTRUCHIO)

BOSOLA You say you would fain be taken for an eminent
courtier?

CASTRUCHIO 'Tis the very main of my ambition.

BOSOLA Let me see, you have a reasonable good face
for't already, and your nightcap expresses your ears   5
sufficient largely; I would have you learn to twirl the
strings of your band with a good grace; and in a set
speech, at th' end of every sentence, to hum, three or
four times, or blow your nose, till it smart again, to recover your memory. When you come to be a president   10
in criminal causes, if you smile upon a prisoner, hang
him, but if you frown upon him, and threaten him, let
him be sure to scape the gallows.

CASTRUCHIO I would be a very merry president, —

BOSOLA Do not sup a nights; 'twill beget you an admir-   15
able wit.

CASTRUCHIO Rather it would make me have a good stomach to quarrel, for they say your roaring boys eat
meat seldom, and that makes them so valiant: but how
shall I know whether the people take me for an emi-   20
nent fellow?

BOSOLA I will teach a trick to know it: give out you lie
a-dying, and if you hear the common people curse you,
be sure you are taken for one of the prime nightcaps.

(*Enter* OLD LADY)

You come from painting now?   25

OLD LADY From what?

BOSOLA Why, from your scurvy face physic: To behold

28 *inclines*   slopes; ups and downs – i.e. wrinkles.

30 *sloughs*   muddy ditches.

   progress   journey.

36 *careening*   the scraping of paint or barnacles from a boat.

36–7 *morphew'd*   blistered, pock-marked.

37 *disembogue*   leave port.

37–8 **There's rough-cast ... plastic**   there's a rough surface underneath your smooth surface. (Some editions have 'plaster' instead of 'plastic'.)

46–7 **Here are ... physician**   Bosola implies that both Castruchio and the Old Lady suffer from venereal disease which is keeping doctors in work.

48 *footcloth*   protective covering worn by the horses of the wealthy.

49 *high-priz'd*   expensive.

49–50 *fall of the leaf*   each autumn.

51 *meditation*   carefully considered thoughts.

61 *ulcerous wolf*   a reference to lupus (Latin: wolf), a chronic disease of the skin, often affecting the face.

   swinish measle   there was thought to be a connection between a skin disease in pigs (swine) and measles.

thee not painted inclines somewhat near a miracle.
These in thy face here, were deep ruts and foul
sloughs, the last progress. There was a lady in France, 30
that having had the smallpox, flayed the skin off her
face, to make it more level; and whereas before she
look'd like a nutmeg grater, after she resembled an
abortive hedgehog.

OLD LADY   Do you call this painting? 35

BOSOLA. No, no but you call it careening of an old morphew'd lady, to make her disembogue again. There's
rough-cast phrase to your plastic.

OLD LADY   It seems you are well acquainted with my
closet? 40

BOSOLA   One would suspect it for a shop of witchcraft, to
find in it the fat of serpents; spawn of snakes, Jews'
spittle, and their young children's ordure, and all these
for the face. I would sooner eat a dead pigeon, taken
from the soles of the feet of one sick of the plague, than 45
kiss one of you fasting. Here are two of you, whose sin
of your youth is the very patrimony of the physician,
makes him renew his footcloth with the spring, and
change his high-priz'd courtesan with the fall of the
leaf: I do wonder you do not loathe yourselves. 50
Observe my meditation now:
What thing is in this outward form of man
To be belov'd? We account it ominous,
If nature do produce a colt, or lamb,
A fawn, or goat, in any limb resembling 55
A man; and fly from't as a prodigy.
Man stands amaz'd to see his deformity,
In any other creature but himself.
But in our own flesh, though we bear diseases
Which have their true names only tane from beasts, 60
As the most ulcerous wolf, and swinish measle;
Though we are eaten up of lice, and worms,
And though continually we bear about us

65 **rich tissue**   fine clothes.

67 **to be made sweet**   i.e. by the process of decay and renewal.

68 **couple**   go together.

69 **well ... aches**   the waters of spas such as Lucca were reputed to cure various ills.

70 **on foot**   in hand, in progress.

72 **fins**   rims.

   teeming   to teem is to be pregnant or to give birth.

77 **apricocks**   apricots.

84 **opinion ... tetter**   reputation for wisdom is a foul disease (a tetter being a skin eruption).

A rotten and dead body, we delight
To hide it in rich tissue: all our fear,   65
Nay, all our terror, is lest our physician
Should put us in the ground, to be made sweet.
Your wife's gone to Rome: you two couple, and get you
To the wells at Lucca, to recover your aches.

(*Exeunt* CASTRUCHIO *and* OLD LADY)

I have other work on foot: I observe our Duchess   70
Is sick a-days, she pukes, her stomach seethes,
The fins of her eyelids look most teeming blue,
She wanes i'th' cheek, and waxes fat i'th' flank;
And, contrary to our Italian fashion,
Wears a loose-bodied gown: there's somewhat in't.   75
I have a trick, may chance discover it,
A pretty one; I have bought some apricocks,
The first our spring yields.

(*Enter* ANTONIO *and* DELIO.)

DELIO   And so long since married?
    You amaze me.
ANTONIO   Let me seal your lips for ever,
    For did I think that anything but th' air   80
    Could carry these words from you, I should wish
    You had no breath at all. (*to* BOSOLA) Now sir, in your
        contemplation?
    You are studying to become a great wise fellow?
BOSOLA   Oh sir, the opinion of wisdom is a foul tetter,
    that runs all over a man's body: if simplicity direct us   85
    to have no evil, it directs us to a happy being. For the
    subtlest folly proceeds from the subtlest wisdom. Let
    me be simply honest.
ANTONIO   I do understand your inside.
BOSOLA   Do you so?   90
ANTONIO   Because you would not seem to appear to
    th' world

49

102 **devil ... th'air**   the devil, or the devil's agents, were reputed to live in the element of air.

103 **ascendant**   your fortune is on the increase (from astrology, where the position of your stars has an influence on your fortunes).

104–5 **cousin-german**   first cousin.

106 **King Pippin**   King of the Franks, father of Charlemagne who ruled an empire centred on what is now France from 742 to 814.

113 **tithe**   a tenth part, a tax paid to the church.

117 **short-winded**   out of breath.

122 **when?**   she is impatient.

123 **lemon peels**   chewed to prevent (or cover up) bad breath.

Puff'd up with your preferment, you continue
This out of fashion melancholy; leave it, leave it.

BOSOLA Give me leave to be honest in any phrase, in
any compliment whatsoever: shall I confess myself to   95
you? I look no higher than I can reach: they are the
gods, that must ride on winged horses; a lawyer's mule
of a slow pace will both suit my disposition and business. For, mark me, when a man's mind rides faster
than his horse can gallop they quickly both tire.   100

ANTONIO You would look up to Heaven, but I think
the devil, that rules i'th' air, stands in your light.

BOSOLA Oh, sir, you are lord of the ascendant, chief
man with the Duchess: a duke was your cousin-
german, remov'd. Say you were lineally descended   105
from King Pippin, or he himself, what of this? Search
the heads of the greatest rivers in the world, you shall
find them but bubbles of water. Some would think the
souls of princes were brought forth by some more
weighty cause, than those of meaner persons; they are   110
deceiv'd, there's the same hand to them: the like passions sway them; the same reason, that makes a vicar
go to law for a tithe-pig, and undo his neighbours,
makes them spoil a whole province, and batter down
goodly cities with the cannon.   115

(*Enter* DUCHESS, OLD LADY, LADIES)

DUCHESS Your arm Antonio, do I not grow fat?
I am exceeding short-winded. Bosola,
I would have you, sir, provide for me a litter,
Such a one, as the Duchess of Florence rode in.

BOSOLA The duchess us'd one, when she was great with
child.   120

DUCHESS I think she did. Come hither, mend my ruff,
Here; when? thou art such a tedious lady; and
Thy breath smells of lemon peels; would thou hadst
done;

124 **sound**   faint.

125 **mother**   a sort of nervous illness which made the sufferer short of breath and liable to faint; also known as smother and sometimes used as a synonym for hysteria.

128 **presence**   the formal audience chamber.

135 **bare**   bare-headed; removing a hat was (and is) a sign of deference.

139 **to-year**   this year.

143 **pare**   peel, skin.

144 **musk**   strong smelling substance used in perfume.

Shall I sound under thy fingers? I am
So troubled with the mother.
BOSOLA (*aside*)   I fear too much.   125
DUCHESS   I have heard you say that the French courtiers
Wear their hats on 'fore the king.
ANTONIO   I have seen it.
DUCHESS   In the presence?
ANTONIO   Yes.
DUCHESS   Why should not we bring up that fashion?
'Tis ceremony more than duty, that consists   130
In the removing of a piece of felt:
Be you the example to the rest o'th' court,
Put on your hat first.
ANTONIO   You must pardon me:
I have seen, in colder countries than in France,
Nobles stand bare to th' prince; and the distinction   135
Methought show'd reverently.
BOSOLA   I have a present for your Grace.
DUCHESS   For me sir?
BOSOLA   Apricocks, Madam.
DUCHESS   O sir, where are they?
I have heard of none to-year.
BOSOLA (*aside*)   Good, her colour rises.
DUCHESS   Indeed I thank you: they are wondrous fair
ones.   140
What an unskilful fellow is our gardener!
We shall have none this month.
BOSOLA   Will not your Grace pare them?
DUCHESS   No, they taste of musk, methinks; indeed they
do.
BOSOLA   I know not: yet I wish your Grace had par'd
'em.   145
DUCHESS   Why?
BOSOLA   I forgot to tell you the knave gard'ner,
Only to raise his profit by them the sooner,
Did ripen them in horse-dung.

150–1 **you are loth ... dainties**   you don't want to take the delicacies away
from me.

153 **grafting**   a horticultural technique which involves growing a delicate
plant on the root and stem of a common, more robust one. There is an
obvious reference here to the Duchess's marriage to Antonio and her
subsequent pregnancy.

154 **pippin**   a variety of apple.

crab   crab-apple.

156 **bawd farthingales**   hooped petticoats which disguise pregnancy and
therefore hide sexual misconduct.

159 **springal**   young animal, lively youth.

cutting a caper   dancing, bouncing.

169 **remove**   removal, escape.

DUCHESS   Oh you jest.
(*to* ANTONIO) You shall judge: pray taste one.
ANTONIO   Indeed Madam,
   I do not love the fruit.
DUCHESS   Sir, you are loth   150
   To rob us of our dainties: 'tis a delicate fruit,
   They say they are restorative?
BOSOLA   'Tis a pretty art,
   This grafting.
DUCHESS   'Tis so: a bett'ring of nature.
BOSOLA   To make a pippin grow upon a crab,
   A damson on a black-thorn: (*aside*) How greedily she
      eats them!   155
   A whirlwind strike off these bawd farthingales,
   For, but for that, and the loose-bodied gown,
   I should have discover'd apparently
   The young springal cutting a caper in her belly.
DUCHESS   I thank you, Bosola: they were right good
      ones.   160
   If they do not make me sick.
ANTONIO   How now Madam?
DUCHESS   This green fruit and my stomach are not
      friends.
   How they swell me!
BOSOLA   (*aside*) Nay, you are too much swell'd already.
DUCHESS   Oh, I am in an extreme cold sweat.
BOSOLA   I am very sorry.

                                              Exit

DUCHESS   Lights to my chamber! O, good Antonio,   165
   I fear I am undone.

                                        Exit DUCHESS

DELIO   Lights there, lights!
ANTONIO   O my most trusty Delio, we are lost:
   I fear she's fall'n in labour: and there's left
   No time for her remove.

171 **politic** discreet, secret.

175–6 **give some colour ... close** explanation for her keeping herself private.

1 **tetchiness** irritability.

3 **breeding** pregnancy.

6 **glass-house** glass factory.

DELIO   Have you prepar'd
  Those ladies to attend her? and procur'd   170
  That politic safe conveyance for the midwife
  Your duchess plotted?
ANTONIO   I have.
DELIO   Make use then of this forc'd occasion:
  Give out that Bosola hath poison'd her,
  With these apricocks: that will give some colour   175
  For her keeping close.
ANTONIO   Fie, fie, the physicians
  Will then flock to her.
DELIO   For that you may pretend
  She'll use some prepar'd antidote of her own,
  Lest the physicians should repoison her.
ANTONIO   I am lost in amazement: I know not what to
    think on't.   180

                                       Exeunt

Scene two

(*Enter* BOSOLA *and* OLD LADY)

BOSOLA   So, so: there's no question but her tetchiness
    and most vulturous eating of the apricocks, are appa-
    rent signs of breeding, now?
OLD LADY   I am in haste, sir.
BOSOLA   There was a young waiting-woman, had a mon-   5
    strous desire to see the glass-house —
OLD LADY   Nay, pray let me go:
BOSOLA   And it was only to know what strange instru-
    ment it was, should swell up a glass to the fashion of a
    woman's belly.   10
OLD LADY   I will hear no more of the glass-house, you
    are still abusing women!
BOSOLA   Who, I? no, only, by the way now and then,

14–18 ***The orange ... tastes well***   presumably Bosola implies that women of all ages are equally lascivious.

19–20 ***Jupiter ... Danaes***   see note to Act 1, scene 2, line 171.

24–5 ***Why, to know ... centre***   sex is at the root of everything.

25–6 ***foster-daughters***   Bosola implies she is a madam in charge of prostitutes.

30 ***shut ... presently***   close the gates immediately.

mention your frailties. The orange tree bears ripe and
green fruit and blossoms altogether. And some of you   15
give entertainment for pure love: but more, for more
precious reward. The lusty spring smells well: but
drooping autumn tastes well. If we have the same golden showers, that rained in the time of Jupiter the
Thunderer: you have the same Danaes still, to hold up   20
their laps to receive them: didst thou never study the
mathematics?

OLD LADY What's that, sir?

BOSOLA Why, to know the trick how to make a many
lines meet in one centre. Go, go; give your foster-   25
daughters good counsel: tell them, that the devil takes
delight to hang at a woman's girdle, like a false rusty
watch, that she cannot discern how the time passes.

Exit OLD LADY; *enter* ANTONIO, DELIO, RODERIGO, GRISOLAN

ANTONIO Shut up the court gates.

RODERIGO   Why sir? what's the danger?

ANTONIO Shut up the posterns presently: and call   30
All the officers o'th' court.

GRISOLAN   I shall instantly.

Exit

ANTONIO Who keeps the key o'th' park-gate?

RODERIGO   Forobosco.

ANTONIO Let him bring't presently.

Exit RODERIGO

(*Enter* SERVANTS, GRISOLAN, RODERIGO)

1 SERVANT Oh, gentlemen o'th' court, the foulest
treason!

BOSOLA (*aside*) If that these apricocks should be
poison'd, now;   35
Without my knowledge!

59

36 **taken** arrested.

37 **Switzer** Swiss soldier; Swiss mercenaries frequently served in the private guards of Italian and German states.

38 **cod-piece** addition at the crotch of close-fitting breeches, often ornamented and often the subject of jokes.

46 **plate** tableware, usually of silver.

48 **cabinet** private rooms.

55–6 **She entreats ... by it** she begs you not to be offended. Those who are innocent will gain all the more credit.

59 **black-guard** kitchen servants.

1 SERVANT   There was taken even now
A Switzer in the Duchess' bedchamber.
2 SERVANT   A Switzer?
1 SERVANT   With a pistol in his great cod-piece.
BOSOLA   Ha, ha, ha.
1 SERVANT   The cod-piece was the case for't.
2 SERVANT   There was a cunning traitor.
Who would have search'd his cod-piece?   40
1 SERVANT   True, if he had kept out of the ladies'
    chambers:
And all the moulds of his buttons were leaden bullets.
2 SERVANT   Oh wicked cannibal: a fire-lock in's cod-
    piece?
1 SERVANT   'Twas a French plot upon my life.
2 SERVANT   To see what the devil can do.
ANTONIO   All the officers here?
SERVANTS   We are.
ANTONIO   Gentlemen,   45
We have lost much plate you know; and but this evening
Jewels, to the value of four thousand ducats
Are missing in the Duchess' cabinet.
Are the gates shut?
1 SERVANT   Yes.
ANTONIO   'Tis the Duchess' pleasure
Each officer be lock'd into his chamber   50
Till the sun-rising; and to send the keys
Of all their chests, and of their outward doors
Into her bedchamber. She is very sick.
RODERIGO   At her pleasure.
ANTONIO   She entreats you take't not ill. The innocent   55
Shall be the more approv'd by it.
BOSOLA   Gentleman o'th' wood-yard, where's your
    Switzer now?
1 SERVANT   By this hand 'twas credibly reported by one
o'th' black-guard.

                    Exeunt BOSOLA, RODERIGO *and* SERVANTS

                                                            61

64 **post** hurry.

80 **set a figure ... nativity** calculate a horoscope for the child's birth.

DELIO   How fares it with the Duchess?
ANTONIO   She's expos'd   60
  Unto the worst of torture, pain, and fear.
DELIO   Speak to her all happy comfort.
ANTONIO   How I do play the fool with mine own danger!
  You are this night, dear friend, to post to Rome,
  My life lies in your service.
DELIO   Do not doubt me.   65
ANTONIO   Oh, 'tis far from me: and yet fear presents me
  Somewhat that looks like danger.
DELIO   Believe it,
  'Tis but the shadow of your fear, no more:
  How superstitiously we mind our evils!
  The throwing down salt, or crossing of a hare;   70
  Bleeding at nose, the stumbling of a horse:
  Or singing of a cricket, are of power
  To daunt whole man in us. Sir, fare you well:
  I wish you all the joys of a bless'd father;
  And, for my faith, lay this unto your breast,   75
  Old friends, like old swords, still are trusted best.

Exit DELIO

(*Enter* CARIOLA *with a child*)

CARIOLA   Sir, you are the happy father of a son,
  Your wife commends him to you.
ANTONIO   Blessed comfort!
  For heaven' sake tend her well: I'll presently
  Go set a figure for's nativity.   80

Exeunt

s.d. **dark lanthorn**   lantern which emitted a dim light.

1 *list*   listen.

5 *several wards*   separate rooms.

6 *My intelligence ... else*   my position as spy will be worthless otherwise.

20–1 *I have been ... jewels*   see note to line 80 in scene 2, above. Antonio claims to have been using astrological means to discover the Duchess's missing jewels; there is a secondary meaning to do with calculating their value.

Scene three

(*Enter* BOSOLA *with a dark lanthorn*)

BOSOLA   Sure I did hear a woman shriek: list, ha?
  And the sound came, if I receiv'd it right,
  From the Duchess' lodgings: there's some stratagem
  In the confining all our courtiers
  To their several wards. I must have part of it,   5
  My intelligence will freeze else. List again,
  It may be 'twas the melancholy bird,
  Best friend of silence, and of solitariness,
  The owl, that scream'd so: ha! Antonio?

(*Enter* ANTONIO *with a candle, his sword drawn*)

ANTONIO   I heard some noise: who's there? What art
    thou? Speak.   10
BOSOLA   Antonio! Put not your face nor body
  To such a forc'd expression of fear,
  I am Bosola; your friend.
ANTONIO   Bosola!
  (*aside*) This mole does undermine me – heard you not
    A noise even now?
BOSOLA   From whence?
ANTONIO   From the Duchess' lodging.   15
BOSOLA   Not I: did you?
ANTONIO   I did: or else I dream'd.
BOSOLA   Let's walk towards it.
ANTONIO   No. It may be 'twas
  But the rising of the wind.
BOSOLA   Very likely.
  Methinks 'tis very cold, and yet you sweat.
  You look wildly.
ANTONIO   I have been setting a figure   20
  For the Duchess' jewels.

22 **Do you ... radical?**   does it lead you to something fundamental?

32 **imputation**   implication, suggestion.

34 **In my conceit**   to my way of thinking.

39 **scarce warm**   the reference is to a snake coming out of hibernation, Bosola only relatively recently having been appointed to the household.

BOSOLA   some text is missing here which would explain the following two lines – possibly Bosola offering to put his signature to the horoscope as evidence of his innocence and good will.

44 **Two letters**   Antonio is looking at his handkerchief which is embroidered with his initials.

46–7 **for you, sir ... be safe**   I'll deal with you in the morning.

BOSOLA   Ah: and how falls your question?
  Do you find it radical?
ANTONIO   What's that to you?
  'Tis rather to be question'd what design,
  When all men were commanded to their lodgings,
  Makes you a night-walker.
BOSOLA   In sooth I'll tell you: 25
  Now all the court's asleep, I thought the devil
  Had least to do here; I come to say my prayers,
  And if it do offend you, I do so,
  You are a fine courtier.
ANTONIO (*aside*)   This fellow will undo me.
  You gave the Duchess apricocks to-day,   30
  Pray heaven they were not poison'd!
BOSOLA   Poison'd! a Spanish fig
  For the imputation.
ANTONIO   Traitors are ever confident,
  Till they are discover'd. There were jewels stol'n too,
  In my conceit, none are to be suspected
  More than yourself.
BOSOLA   You are a false steward.   35
ANTONIO   Saucy slave! I'll pull thee up by the roots.
BOSOLA   May be the ruin will crush you to pieces.
ANTONIO   You are an impudent snake indeed, sir,
  Are you scarce warm, and do you show your sting?
BOSOLA   . . .
ANTONIO   You libel well, sir.
BOSOLA   No sir, copy it out: 40
  And I will set my˙hand to't.
ANTONIO   My nose bleeds.
  One that were superstitious, would count
  This ominous: when it merely comes by chance.
  Two letters, that are wrought here for my name
  Are drown'd in blood!   45
  Mere accident: for you, sir, I'll take order:

47 *colour*   cover up, hide.

50 *quit*   acquitted.

54 *false friend*   the dark lanthorn.

58 *decimo nono Decembris*   (Latin) 19 December.

60 *house*   one of the twelve divisions of the heavens in astrology.

   combust   used up, weakened.

63 *Cætera non scrutantur*   the remainder is not clear, cannot be
   deciphered.

65 *bawd*   go-between – i.e. between the Duchess and her lover. He does
   not suspect Antonio of being her lover.

66 *intelligency*   information.

67 *cas'd up*   confined to their rooms.

73–4 *galls ... livers*   bitterness (from gall) will overwhelm their feelings
   (supposed to be situated in the liver).

75 **Though lust ... disguise**   though lust disguises herself in many strange
   ways.

I'th' morn you shall be safe: (*aside*) 'tis that must col-
  our
Her lying-in: sir, this door you pass not:
I do not hold it fit, that you come near
The Duchess' lodgings, till you have quit yourself;   50
(*aside*) *The great are like the base; nay, they are the same,*
When they seek shameful ways to avoid shame.

                                                              Exit

BOSOLA   Antonio here about did drop a paper,
Some of your help, false friend: oh, here it is.
What's here? a child's nativity calculated?   55
(*reads:*) *The Duchess was deliver'd of a son, 'tween the hours*
twelve and one, in the night: Anno Dom: 1504. (*that's this*
year) decimo nono Decembris, (*that's this night*) *taken*
according to the Meridian of Malfi (*that's our Duchess: happy*
discovery). *The Lord of the first house, being combust in the*   60
ascendant, signifies short life: and Mars *being in a human*
sign, join'd to the tail of the Dragon, in the eighth house, doth
threaten a violent death; Cætera non scrutantur.
Why now 'tis most apparent. This precise fellow
Is the Duchess' bawd: I have it to my wish.   65
This is a parcel of intelligency
Our courtiers were cas'd up for! It needs must follow,
That I must be committed, on pretence
Of poisoning her: which I'll endure, and laugh at.
If one could find the father now: but that   70
Time will discover. Old Castruchio
I'th' morning posts to Rome; by him I'll send
A letter, that shall make her brothers' galls
O'erflow their livers. This was a thrifty way.
Though lust do masque in ne'er so strange disguise   75
She's oft found witty, but is never wise.

                                                              Exit

4 **anchorite** holy woman, often a hermit.

6 **I mean to him** I mean, you are false to him.

11 **approv'd** felt.

13–15 **Sooth ... them fixed** you are as likely to be able to bend glass as to find a woman who is constant.

16 **fantastic glass** Galileo's telescope – though, in 1504 (see line 57 in scene 3, above) it had not yet been invented!

Scene four

(*Enter* CARDINAL *and* JULIA)

CARDINAL   Sit: thou art my best of wishes; prithee tell
    me
  What trick didst thou invent to come to Rome,
  Without thy husband?

JULIA   Why, my Lord, I told him
  I came to visit an old anchorite
  Here, for devotion.

CARDINAL   Thou art a witty false one: 5
  I mean to him.

JULIA   You have prevailed with me
  Beyond my strongest thoughts: I would not now
  Find you inconstant.

CARDINAL   Do not put thyself
  To such a voluntary torture, which proceeds
  Out of your own guilt.

JULIA   How, my Lord?

CARDINAL   You fear   10
  My constancy, because you have approv'd
  Those giddy and wild turnings in yourself.

JULIA   Did you e'er find them?

CARDINAL   Sooth, generally for women;
  A man might strive to make glass malleable,
  Ere he should make them fixed.

JULIA   So, my Lord.   15

CARDINAL   We had need go borrow that fantastic glass
  Invented by Galileo the Florentine,
  To view another spacious world i'th' moon,
  And look to find a constant woman there.

JULIA   This is very well, my Lord.

CARDINAL   Why do you weep?   20
  Are tears your justification? The selfsame tears
  Will fall into your husband's bosom, lady,

25 *jealously*   fiercely.

26 *cuckold*   being unmarried, the Cardinal cannot ever be a cuckold (i.e. someone whose wife is unfaithful).

28–30 *perch ... fly at it*   the Cardinal compares Julia to a falcon.

39 *in physic*   under medical attention.

41 *to't*   to it, i.e. compared to it.

45 *post*   swiftly.

With a loud protestation that you love him
Above the world. Come, I'll love you wisely,
That's jealously, since I am very certain   25
You cannot me make cuckold.
JULIA   I'll go home
To my husband.
CARDINAL   You may thank me, lady,
I have taken you off your melancholy perch,
Bore you upon my fist, and show'd you game,
And let you fly at it. I pray thee kiss me.   30
When thou wast with thy husband, thou wast watch'd
Like a tame elephant: (still you are to thank me.)
Thou hadst only kisses from him, and high feeding,
But what delight was that? 'Twas just like one
That hath a little fing'ring on the lute,   35
Yet cannot tune it: (still you are to thank me.)
JULIA   You told me of a piteous wound i'th' heart,
And a sick liver, when you wooed me first,
And spake like one in physic.
CARDINAL   Who's that?

(*Enter* SERVANT)

Rest firm, for my affection to thee,   40
Lightning moves slow to't.
SERVANT   Madam, a gentleman
That's come post from Malfi, desires to see you.
CARDINAL   Let him enter, I'll withdraw.

                                                              Exit

SERVANT   He says
Your husband, old Castruchio, is come to Rome,
Most pitifully tir'd with riding post.   45

                        (*Exit* SERVANT; *enter* DELIO)

JULIA   Signior Delio! (*aside*) 'tis one of my old suitors.
DELIO   I was bold to come and see you.

                                                                73

48 **lie**   lodge, stay.

56 **breach**   backside.

57 **Is my pity**   makes me feel sorry for him.

64 **cassia**   a spice.

   civet   strong perfume.

65 **physical**   medicinal.

   fond   foolish.

66 **seethe't in cullises**   boil it in medicinal broths.

68 **Duke of Calabria**   Ferdinand.

JULIA   Sir, you are welcome.

DELIO   Do you lie here?

JULIA   Sure, your own experience
   Will satisfy you no; our Roman prelates
   Do not keep lodging for ladies.

DELIO   Very well.   50
   I have brought you no commendations from your hus-
     band,
   For I know none by him.

JULIA   I hear he's come to Rome?

DELIO   I never knew man and beast, of a horse and a
     knight,
   So weary of each other; if he had had a good back,
   He would have undertook to have borne his horse,   55
   His breach was so pitifully sore.

JULIA   Your laughter
   Is my pity.

DELIO   Lady, I know not whether
   You want money, but I have brought you some.

JULIA   From my husband?

DELIO   No, from mine own allowance.

JULIA   I must hear the condition, ere I be bound to take it.   60

DELIO   Look on't, 'tis gold, hath it not a fine colour?

JULIA   I have a bird more beautiful.

DELIO   Try the sound on't.

JULIA   A lute-string far exceeds it;
   It hath no smell, like cassia or civet,
   Nor is it physical, though some fond doctors   65
   Persuade us, seethe't in cullises. I'll tell you,
   This is a creature bred by —

(*Enter* SERVANT)

SERVANT   Your husband's come,
   Hath deliver'd a letter to the Duke of Calabria,
   That, to my thinking, hath put him out of his wits.

                            Exit SERVANT

                                        75

71 *suit*   point, purpose.

77 *honesty*   chastity.

82–3 **They ... action's done**   those who do not consider things thoroughly beforehand bring misfortunes on themselves.

1 *mandrake*   a poisonous plant to which many superstitions were attached. One belief was that the plant shrieked when pulled up and drove the hearer mad.

2 *prodigy*   outcome.

3 *loose, i'th'hilts*   promiscuous.

6 *bounty*   generosity.

JULIA   Sir, you hear,   70
  Pray let me know your business and your suit,
  As briefly as can be.
DELIO   With good speed. I would wish you,
  At such time, as you are non-resident
  With your husband, my mistress.
JULIA   Sir, I'll go ask my husband if I shall,   75
  And straight return your answer.

Exit

DELIO   Very fine,
  Is this her wit, or honesty that speaks thus?
  I heard one say the Duke was highly mov'd
  With a letter sent from Malfi. I do fear
  Antonio is betray'd: how fearfully   80
  Shows his ambition now; unfortunate Fortune!
  They pass through whirlpools, and deep woes do shun,
  Who the event weigh, ere the action's done.

Exit

Scene five

(*Enter* CARDINAL, *and* FERDINAND, *with a letter*)

FERDINAND   I have this night digg'd up a mandrake.
CARDINAL   Say you?
FERDINAND   And I am grown mad with't.
CARDINAL   What's the prodigy?
FERDINAND   Read there, a sister damn'd, she's loose, i'th'
  hilts:
  Grown a notorious strumpet.
CARDINAL   Speak lower.
FERDINAND   Lower?
  Rogues do not whisper't now, but seek to publish't,   5
  As servants do the bounty of their lords,

7 **covetous**   hoping for gain.

9 **bawds**   go-betweens, procurers.

10–11 **And more ... service**   she has more ways of satisfying her lust than garrison towns have of securing supplies; service has an additional implication of sexual activity.

12–13 **Rhubarb ... choler**   rhubarb was used as a medicine, especially to deal with an excess of choler. Choler (yellow bile) was one of the four humours of medieval and subsequent medical theory. A choleric person was angry and irritable.

13 **cursed day**   presumably the day of the Duchess's child's birth.

19 **blast her meads**   flatten her fields as with a hurricane.

21 **our blood**   our family honour.

23 **attainted**   tainted, stained.

24 **balsamum**   healing ointment.

25 **cupping-glass**   used as a tool to draw blood from a patient in the medicinal practice of blood-letting; this was a painful and desperate 'remedy'.

   mean   means, way.

32 **Unequal**   unjust.

33 **left side**   the left side was felt to be the wrong side; in Latin, left is *sinistra* from which we derive sinister.

Aloud; and with a covetous searching eye,
To mark who note them. Oh confusion seize her,
She hath had most cunning bawds to serve her turn,
And more secure conveyances for lust,   10
Than towns of garrison, for service.
CARDINAL   Is't possible?
Can this be certain?
FERDINAND   Rhubarb, oh for rhubarb
To purge this choler; here's the cursed day
To prompt my memory, and here't shall stick
Till of her bleeding heart I make a sponge   15
To wipe it out.
CARDINAL   Why do you make yourself
So wild a tempest?
FERDINAND   Would I could be one,
That I might toss her palace 'bout her ears,
Root up her goodly forests, blast her meads,
And lay her general territory as waste,   20
As she hath done her honour's.
CARDINAL   Shall our blood?
The royal blood of Aragon and Castile,
Be thus attainted?
FERDINAND   Apply desperate physic,
We must not now use balsamum, but fire,
The smarting cupping-glass, for that's the mean   25
To purge infected blood, such blood as hers.
There is a kind of pity in mine eye,
I'll give it to my handkercher; and now 'tis here,
I'll bequeath this to her bastard.
CARDINAL   What to do?
FERDINAND Why, to make soft lint for his mother's
    wounds,   30
When I have hewed her to pieces.
CARDINAL   Curs'd creature!
Unequal nature, to place women's hearts
So far upon the left side.

34 **bark** boat.

37 **purchas'd** gained.

43 **happily** perhaps.

44 **quoit the sledge** toss the sledgehammer.

45 **lovely** outwardly attractive.

46 **privy** private.

48 **wild-fire** skin disease; also fire employed in warfare which is hard to extinguish.

56 **palsy** affliction.

57 **rupture** rapture, passion.

60 **You have divers** there are many.

FERDINAND   Foolish men,
  That e'er will trust their honour in a bark,
  Made of so slight, weak bulrush, as is woman,   35
  Apt every minute to sink it!
CARDINAL   Thus ignorance, when it hath purchas'd hon-
    our,
  It cannot wield it.
FERDINAND   Methinks I see her laughing,
  Excellent hyena! Talk to me somewhat, quickly,
  Or my imagination will carry me   40
  To see her in the shameful act of sin.
CARDINAL   With whom?
FERDINAND   Happily, with·some strong thigh'd barge-
    man;
  Or one o'th' wood-yard, that can quoit the sledge
  Or toss the bar, or else some lovely squire   45
  That carries coals up to her privy lodgings.
CARDINAL   You fly beyond your reason.
FERDINAND   Go to, mistress!
  'Tis not your whore's milk, that shall quench my wild-
    fire
  But your whore's blood.
CARDINAL   How idly shows this rage! which carries you,   50
  As men convey'd by witches, through the air
  On violent whirlwinds: this intemperate noise
  Fitly resembles deaf men's shrill discourse,
  Who talk aloud, thinking all other men
  To have their imperfection.
FERDINAND   Have not you   55
  My palsy?
CARDINAL   Yes, I can be angry
  Without this rupture; there is not in nature
  A thing, that makes man so deform'd, so beastly
  As doth intemperate anger; chide yourself:
  You have divers men, who never yet express'd   60
  Their strong desire of rest but by unrest,

68 **ventage**   vent, air passage.

72 **cullis**   stew, broth.

74 **The sin of his back**   his lechery.

78 **Till I know ... stir**   I'll do nothing until I know who is my sister's lover.

79 **scorpions**   pieces of sharp steel fixed to the thongs of a whip.

80 **general eclipse**   total annihilation.

By vexing of themselves. Come, put yourself
In tune.

FERDINAND   So, I will only study to seem
The thing I am not. I could kill her now,
In you, or in myself, for I do think   65
It is some sin in us, Heaven doth revenge
By her.

CARDINAL   Are you stark mad?

FERDINAND   I would have their bodies
Burnt in a coal-pit, with the ventage stopp'd,
That their curs'd smoke might not ascend to Heaven:
Or dip the sheets they lie in, in pitch or sulphur,   70
Wrap them in't, and then light them like a match:
Or else to boil their bastard to a cullis,
And give't his lecherous father, to renew
The sin of his back.

CARDINAL   I'll leave you.

FERDINAND   Nay, I have done;
I am confident, had I been damn'd in hell,   75
And should have heard of this, it would have put me
Into a cold sweat. In, in, I'll go sleep:
Till I know who leaps my sister, I'll not stir:
That known, I'll find scorpions to string my whips,
And fix her in a general eclipse.   80

Exeunt

6 **Feeder of pedigrees** breeder.

14 **reversion** inheritance.

19 **bear** behave.

24 **Till the devil be up** until the devil is about, awakened.

Act Three

Scene one

(*Enter* ANTONIO *and* DELIO)

ANTONIO Our noble friend, my most beloved Delio,
   Oh, you have been a stranger long at court,
   Came you along with the Lord Ferdinand?
DELIO I did, sir, and how fares your noble Duchess?
ANTONIO Right fortunately well. She's an excellent   5
   Feeder of pedigrees: since you last saw her,
   She hath had two children more, a son and daughter.
DELIO Methinks 'twas yesterday. Let me but wink,
   And not behold your face, which to mine eye
   Is somewhat leaner: verily I should dream   10
   It were within this half hour.
ANTONIO You have not been in law, friend Delio,
   Nor in prison, nor a suitor at the court,
   Nor begg'd the reversion of some great man's place,
   Nor troubled with an old wife, which doth make   15
   Your time so insensibly hasten.
DELIO   Pray sir tell me,
   Hath not this news arriv'd yet to the ear
   Of the Lord Cardinal?
ANTONIO   I fear it hath;
   The Lord Ferdinand, that's newly come to court,
   Doth bear himself right dangerously.
DELIO   Pray why?   20
ANTONIO He is so quiet, that he seems to sleep
   The tempest out, as dormice do in winter;
   Those houses, that are haunted, are most still,
   Till the devil be up.
DELIO   What say the common people?
ANTONIO The common rabble do directly say   25
   She is a strumpet.

26 **graver heads**   calmer, wiser people.

27 **politic**   tactful.

   censure they   opinion do they have.

28–9 **They do ... way**   they observe that I seem to enrich myself by underhand means.

34 **odious**   unpopular.

39 **bespeak**   arrange.

42 **stick of sugar-candy**   someone of outward appearance without any depth, someone whom one could 'see through'.

49 **Pasquil**   a character with a sharp tongue; a statue named after him in Rome became a place where people put up satirical verse and other 'paper bullets'.

   calumny   slander.

51 **Are seldom purg'd of**   are rarely completely free of.

52 **I pour it in your bosom**   I tell you confidentially.

DELIO   And your graver heads,
  Which would be politic, what censure they?
ANTONIO   They do observe I grow to infinite purchase
  The left-hand way, and all suppose the Duchess
  Would amend it, if she could. For, say they,   30
  Great princes, though they grudge their officers
  Should have such large and unconfined means
  To get wealth under them, will not complain
  Lest thereby they should make them odious
  Unto the people: for other obligation   35
  Of love, or marriage, between her and me,
  They never dream of.

(*Enter* FERDINAND, DUCHESS *and* BOSOLA)

DELIO   The Lord Ferdinand
  Is going to bed.
FERDINAND   I'll instantly to bed,
  For I am weary: I am to bespeak
  A husband for you.
DUCHESS   For me, sir! pray who is't?   40
FERDINAND   The great Count Malateste.
DUCHESS   Fie upon him,
  A count? He's a mere stick of sugar-candy,
  You may look quite through him: when I choose
  A husband, I will marry for your honour.
FERDINAND   You shall do well in't. How is't, worthy
    Antonio?   45
DUCHESS   But, sir, I am to have private conference with
    you,
  About a scandalous report is spread
  Touching mine honour.
FERDINAND   Let me be ever deaf to't:
  One of Pasquil's paper bullets, court calumny,
  A pestilent air, which princes' palaces   50
  Are seldom purg'd of. Yet, say that it were true,
  I pour it in your bosom, my fix'd love

53 **extenuate**   reduce.

57 **cultures**   blades of the plough; walking on hot plough shares was a traditional way of putting women accused of unchastity to trial by ordeal.

66 **faith**   superstition.

70 **gulleries**   tricks.

71 **mountebanks**   tricksters, con-men.

73 **force the will**   make people do what they don't want to do.

75 **lenative poisons**   aphrodisiacs.

76 **the witch**   the woman.

77 **equivocation**   twisting logic.

78 **lies ... rank blood**   resides in her corrupt character.

Would strongly excuse, extenuate, nay deny
Faults were they apparent in you. Go, be safe
In your own innocency.
DUCHESS   Oh bless'd comfort,   55
This deadly air is purg'd.

                 Exeunt DUCHESS, ANTONIO, DELIO

FERDINAND   Her guilt treads on
Hot burning cultures. Now Bosola,
How thrives our intelligence?
BOSOLA   Sir, uncertainly:
'Tis rumour'd she hath had three bastards, but
By whom, we may go read i'th' stars.
FERDINAND   Why some   60
Hold opinion, all things are written there.
BOSOLA Yes, if we could find spectacles to read them;
I do suspect, there hath been some sorcery
Us'd on the Duchess.
FERDINAND   Sorcery, to what purpose?
BOSOLA To make her dote on some desertless fellow,   65
She shames to acknowledge.
FERDINAND   Can your faith give way
To think there's power in potions, or in charms,
To make us love, whether we will or no?
BOSOLA Most certainly.
FERDINAND Away, these are mere gulleries, horrid
    things   70
Invented by some cheating mountebanks
To abuse us. Do you think that herbs, or charms
Can force the will? Some trials have been made
In the foolish practice; but the ingredients
Were lenative poisons, such as are of force   75
To make the patient mad; and straight the witch
Swears, by equivocation, they are in love.
The witchcraft lies in her rank blood: this night
I will force confession from her. You told me

84 **compass ... drifts**   know all about me.

86 **sounded**   found the depth of.

87–8 **That you/Are ... much**   you blow your own trumpet too much.

90–1 **I never ... flatterers**   until now I only employed flatterers.

92–4 **That friend ... defects**   someone who tells a great man the truth about himself is likely to help him to avoid misfortune.

5 **with cap and knee**   cap in hand and on bended knee.

You had got, within these two days, a false key   80
  Into her bed-chamber.
BOSOLA   I have.
FERDINAND   As I would wish.
BOSOLA   What do you intend to do?
FERDINAND   Can you guess?
BOSOLA   No.
FERDINAND   Do not ask then.
  He that can compass me, and know my drifts,
  May say he hath put a girdle 'bout the world,   85
  And sounded all her quick-sands.
BOSOLA   I do not
  Think so.
FERDINAND   What do you think then, pray?
BOSOLA   That you
  Are your own chronicle too much: and grossly
  Flatter yourself.
FERDINAND   Give me thy hand: I thank thee.
  I never gave pension but to flatterers,   90
  Till I entertained thee: farewell,
  That friend a great man's ruin strongly checks,
  Who rails into his belief all his defects.

                         Exeunt

Scene two

(*Enter* DUCHESS, ANTONIO *and* CARIOLA)

DUCHESS   Bring me the casket hither, and the glass;
  You get no lodging here to-night, my lord.
ANTONIO   Indeed, I must persuade one.
DUCHESS   Very good:
  I hope in time 'twill grow into a custom,
  That noblemen shall come with cap and knee,   5
  To purchase a night's lodging of their wives.

7 **lord of mis-rule**   the title given to a person of lower rank who presided over celebrations at festivities (such as Christmas) when the normal social order was reversed.

20 **stop**   close, as in put a stopper in a bottle.

21 **Venus**   the goddess of love who, according to mythology, travelled in a chariot drawn by doves.

25 **peevish**   petulant.

25–32 **Daphne ... eminent stars**   Antonio compares women from legends who rejected male partners with those who married. The former are associated with barrenness and sterility, the latter with growth, fruitfulness and beauty.

33 **vain poetry**   pointless stories.

ANTONIO   I must lie here.
DUCHESS   Must? you are a lord of mis-rule.
ANTONIO   Indeed, my rule is only in the night.
DUCHESS   To what use will you put me?
ANTONIO   We'll sleep together.
DUCHESS   Alas, what pleasure can two lovers find in
  sleep?   10
CARIOLA   My lord, I lie with her often: and I know
  She'll much disquiet you.
ANTONIO   See, you are complain'd of.
CARIOLA   For she's the sprawling'st bedfellow.
ANTONIO   I shall like her the better for that.
CARIOLA   Sir, shall I ask you a question?   15
ANTONIO   I pray thee Cariola.
CARIOLA   Wherefore still, when you lie with my lady
  Do you rise so early?
ANTONIO   Labouring men,
  Count the clock oft'nest Cariola,
  Are glad when their task's ended.
DUCHESS   I'll stop your mouth (*kisses him*).   20
ANTONIO   Nay, that's but one, Venus had two soft doves
  To draw her chariot: I must have another (*kisses her*).
  When wilt thou marry, Cariola?
CARIOLA   Never, my lord.
ANTONIO   O fie upon this single life; forgo it.
  We read how Daphne, for her peevish flight   25
  Became a fruitless bay-tree; Sirinx turn'd
  To the pale empty reed; Anaxarete
  Was frozen into marble: whereas those
  Which married, or prov'd kind unto their friends
  Were, by a gracious influence, transhap'd   30
  Into the olive, pomegranate, mulberry:
  Became flowers, precious stones, or eminent stars.
CARIOLA   This is vain poetry: but I pray you tell me,
  If there were propos'd me wisdom, riches, and beauty,
  In three several young men, which should I choose?   35

36 **Paris** Paris had to judge the relative beauty of three goddesses – not an easy task!

40–2 **'Twas a motion ... Europe** it was a display that would cloud the judgement of the most rigorous judge.

45 **hard favour'd** ugly.

54 **steal forth** creep out of.

55–6 **I have divers ... like** have often done this.

56 **chaf'd extremely** been very annoyed.

58 **'gin** begin.

59 **wax** grow.

60 **arras** a root from which perfume is made.

62 **vouchsafe** agree.

ANTONIO   'Tis a hard question. This was Paris' case
   And he was blind in't, and there was great cause:
   For how was't possible he could judge right,
   Having three amorous goddesses in view,
   And they stark naked? 'Twas a motion   40
   Were able to benight the apprehension
   Of the severest counsellor of Europe.
   Now I look on both your faces, so well form'd
   It puts me in mind of a question, I would ask.
CARIOLA   What is't?
ANTONIO   I do wonder why hard favour'd ladies   45
   For the most part, keep worse-favour'd waiting-
     women,
   To attend them, and cannot endure fair ones.
DUCHESS   Oh, that's soon answer'd.
   Did you ever in your life know an ill painter
   Desire to have his dwelling next door to the shop   50
   Of an excellent picture-maker? 'Twould disgrace
   His face-making, and undo him. I prithee
   When were we so merry? My hair tangles.
ANTONIO   (*aside to* CARIOLA) Pray thee, Cariola, let's
    steal forth the room,
   And let her talk to herself: I have divers times   55
   Serv'd her the like, when she hath chaf'd extremely.
   I love to see her angry: softly Cariola.

                    Exeunt ANTONIO *and* CARIOLA

DUCHESS   Doth not the colour of my hair 'gin to change?
   When I wax grey, I shall have all the court
   Powder their hair with arras, to be like me: 60
   You have cause to love me, I ent'red you into my
    heart

(*Enter* FERDINAND, *unseen*)

   Before you would vouchsafe to call for the keys.
   We shall one day have my brothers take you napping.

68 **gossips** godparents.

s.d. **poniard** dagger.

73 **eclipse thee** hide you, i.e. virtue.

74 **a bare name** i.e. virtue is merely a name, nothing more.

81–2 **there's ... of shame** the only way of dealing with shame is to become so shameless that one is beyond caring about it.

84 **Happily** perhaps.

88 **basilisk** mythical creature whose breath and look were reputed to be fatal.

Methinks his presence, being now in court,
Should make you keep your own bed: but you'll say   65
Love mix'd with fear is sweetest. I'll assure you
You shall get no more children till my brothers
Consent to be your gossips. Have you lost your tongue?

(*She sees* FERDINAND *holding a poniard.*)

'Tis welcome:
For know, whether I am doom'd to live, or die,   70
I can do both like a prince.

(FERDINAND *gives her a poniard.*)

FERDINAND   Die then, quickly.
Virtue, where art thou hid? What hideous thing
Is it, that doth eclipse thee?
DUCHESS   Pray sir hear me —
FERDINAND   Or is it true, thou art but a bare name,
And no essential thing?
DUCHESS   Sir —
FERDINAND   Do not speak.   75
DUCHESS   No sir:
I will plant my soul in mine ears, to hear you.
FERDINAND   Oh most imperfect light of human reason,
That mak'st us so unhappy, to foresee
What we can least prevent. Pursue thy wishes: 80
And glory in them: there's in shame no comfort,
But to be past all bounds and sense of shame.
DUCHESS   I pray sir, hear me: I am married —
FERDINAND   So.
DUCHESS   Happily, not to your liking: but for that
Alas: your shears do come untimely now   85
To clip the bird's wings, that's already flown.
Will you see my husband?
FERDINAND   Yes, if I could change
Eyes with a basilisk.

89 **confederacy** in league with a basilisk.

91 **thou** this is addressed to the Duchess's husband.

100 **vild** vile.

103–4 **as our anchorites ... inhabit** such as holy women hermits inhabit for a holier purpose.

108 **paraquito** parrot.

110 **bewray** betray.

113 **thou hast tane ... lead** you have taken the lead lining of your husband's coffin.

116 **bullet** cannon ball.

117 **wild-fire** see note to Act 2, scene 5, line 48.

DUCHESS   Sure, you came hither
   By his confederacy.
FERDINAND   The howling of a wolf
   Is music to thee, screech-owl; prithee peace.   90
   Whate'er thou art, that hast enjoy'd my sister,
   (For I am sure thou hear'st me), for thine own sake
   Let me not know thee. I came hither prepar'd
   To work thy discovery: yet am now persuaded
   It would beget such violent effects   95
   As would damn us both. I would not for ten millions
   I had beheld thee; therefore use all means
   I never may have knowledge of thy name;
   Enjoy thy lust still, and a wretched life,
   On that condition. And for thee, vild woman,   100
   If thou do wish thy lecher may grow old
   In thy embracements, I would have thee build
   Such a room for him, as our anchorites
   To holier use inhabit. Let not the sun
   Shine on him, till he's dead. Let dogs and monkeys   105
   Only converse with him, and such dumb things
   To whom nature denies use to sound his name.
   Do not keep a paraquito, lest she learn it;
   If thou do love him, cut out thine own tongue
   Lest it bewray him.
DUCHESS   Why might not I marry?   110
   I have not gone about, in this, to create
   Any new world, or custom.
FERDINAND   Thou art undone:
   And thou hast tane that massy sheet of lead
   That hid thy husband's bones, and folded it
   About my heart.
DUCHESS   Mine bleeds for't.
FERDINAND   Thine? thy heart?   115
   What should I name't, unless a hollow bullet
   Fill'd with unquenchable wild-fire?

119 **wilful** obstinate.

135 **shook hands with** said goodbye to.

139 **cas'd up** hidden away.

140 **you have** there are.

142 **apparition** literally, thing that appeared.

DUCHESS   You are in this
  Too strict: and were you not my princely brother
  I would say too wilful. My reputation
  Is safe.
FERDINAND   Dost thou know what reputation is?   120
  I'll tell thee, to small purpose, since th'instruction
  Comes now too late:
  Upon a time Reputation, Love and Death
  Would travel o'er the world: and it was concluded
  That they should part, and take three several ways.   125
  Death told them, they should find him in great battles:
  Or cities plagu'd with plagues. Love gives them
     counsel
  To inquire for him 'mongst unambitious shepherds,
  Where dowries were not talk'd of: and sometimes
  'Mongst quiet kindred, that had nothing left   130
  By their dead parents. 'Stay', quoth Reputation,
  'Do not forsake me: for it is my nature
  If once I part from any man I meet
  I am never found again.' And so, for you:
  You have shook hands with Reputation,   135
  And made him invisible. So fare you well.
  I will never see you more.
DUCHESS   Why should only I,
  Of all the other princes of the world
  Be cas'd up, like a holy relic? I have youth,
  And a little beauty.
FERDINAND   So you have some virgins,   140
  That are witches. I will never see thee more.

                                      Exit

(*Enter* CARIOLA *and* ANTONIO *with a pistol*)

DUCHESS   You saw this apparition?
ANTONIO   Yes: we are
  Betray'd; how came he hither? I should turn
  This, to thee, for that. (*points the pistol at* CARIOLA)

149 **warrantable** lawfully approved.

154 **gall** the gall bladder was associated with bitterness and with haughtiness; in modern usage 'gall' equals cheek.

159 **masks and curtains** deceptions.

160 **fashion'd** organised.

CARIOLA   Pray sir do: and when
   That you have cleft my heart, you shall read there,   145
   Mine innocence.
DUCHESS   That gallery gave him entrance.
ANTONIO   I would this terrible thing would come again,
   That, standing on my guard, I might relate
   My warrantable love. Ha! what means this?
DUCHESS   He left this with me. (*she shows the poniard*)
ANTONIO   And it seems, did wish   150
   You would use it on yourself?
DUCHESS   His action seem'd
   To intend so much.
ANTONIO   This hath a handle to't,
   As well as a point: turn it towards him, and
   So fasten the keen edge in his rank gall. (*knocking*)
   How now? Who knocks? More earthquakes?
DUCHESS   I stand   155
   As if a mine, beneath my feet, were ready
   To be blown up.
CARIOLA   'Tis Bosola.
DUCHESS   Away!
   Oh misery, methinks unjust actions
   Should wear these masks and curtains; and not we.
   You must instantly part hence: I have fashion'd it
      already.   160

                          (*Exit* ANTONIO; *enter* BOSOLA)

BOSOLA   The Duke your brother is tane up in a whirl-
      wind;
   Hath took horse, and's rid post to Rome.
DUCHESS   So late?
BOSOLA   He told me, as he mounted into th' saddle,
   You were undone.
DUCHESS   Indeed, I am very near it.
BOSOLA   What's the matter?   165
DUCHESS   Antonio, the master of our household

                                                            103

168–70 **My brother ... forfeit**   Antonio has failed to repay a loan taken out by the Duchess for which Ferdinand offered security. This is all a deception. She is playing for time.

172 **bills**   IOUs.

protested   rejected.

177 **enginous wheels**   small movements, as in clockwork, producing larger effects.

178 **Must stand for periods**   must do instead of sentences.

179 **Tasso**   (1544–95) Italian poet.

187 **Quietus**   see note to Act 1, scene 2, line 383.

190 **let him**   let him go.

193 **publish**   publicise.

Hath dealt so falsely with me, in's accounts:
My brother stood engag'd with me for money
Tane up of certain Neapolitan Jews,
And Antonio lets the bonds be forfeit.   170
BOSOLA   Strange: (*aside*) this is cunning.
DUCHESS   And hereupon
My brother's bills at Naples are protested
Against. Call up our officers.
BOSOLA   I shall.

                                                    Exit

(*Enter* ANTONIO)

DUCHESS   The place that you must fly to, is Ancona,
Hire a house there. I'll send after you   175
My treasure, and my jewels: our weak safety
Runs upon enginous wheels: short syllables
Must stand for periods. I must now accuse you
Of such a feigned crime, as Tasso calls
Magnanima mensogna: a noble lie,   180
'Cause it must shield our honours: hark, they are com-
    ing.

(*Enter* BOSOLA *and* OFFICERS)

ANTONIO   Will your Grace hear me?
DUCHESS   I have got well by you: you have yielded me
A million of loss; I am like to inherit
The people's curses for your stewardship.   185
You had the trick, in audit time to be sick,
Till I had sign'd your *Quietus*; and that cur'd you
Without help of a doctor. Gentlemen,
I would have this man be an example to you all:
So shall you hold my favour. I pray let him;   190
For h'as done that, alas! you would not think of,
And, because I intend to be rid of him,
I mean not to publish. Use your fortune elsewhere.

194 **brook**   withstand.

197 **necessity ... star**   Antonio blames it all on the influence of the stars.

206 **pass**   permission to go.

209 **extortion**   corruption, using position for gain.

214 **pig's head**   possibly a suggestion that Antonio, in his dislike of pork, has Jewish characteristics.

221 **hermaphrodite**   both male and female.

ANTONIO I am strongly arm'd to brook my overthrow,
As commonly men bear with a hard year: 195
I will not blame the cause on't; but do think
The necessity of my malevolent star
Procures this, not her humour. O the inconstant
And rotten ground of service, you may see;
'Tis ev'n like him that, in a winter night,   200
Takes a long slumber, o'er a dying fire
As loth to part from't: yet parts thence as cold,
As when he first sat down.
DUCHESS   We do confiscate,
Towards the satisfying of your accounts,
All that you have.
ANTONIO   I am all yours; and 'tis very fit   205
All mine should be so.
DUCHESS   So, sir; you have your pass.
ANTONIO You may see, gentlemen, what 'tis to serve
A prince with body and soul.

Exit

BOSOLA Here's an example for extortion; what moisture
is drawn out of the sea, when foul weather comes,   210
pours down, and runs into the sea again.
DUCHESS I would know what are your opinions
Of this Antonio.
2 OFFICER He could not abide to see a pig's head gap-
ing,
I thought your Grace would find him a Jew.   215
3 OFFICER I would you had been his officer, for your
own sake.
4 OFFICER You would have had more money.
1 OFFICER He stopp'd his ears with black wool: and to those
came to him for money said he was thick of hearing. 220
2 OFFICER Some said he was an hermaphrodite, for he
could not abide a woman.

225–6 **chippings ... chain** crusts of bread used to polish metal.

226 **chain** chain of office, i.e. as steward of the household.

228–35 **That these ... livery** i.e. men who would have done anything for him when he was in office, when his fortune was at its height.

231 **in a ring** led by a ring through the nose.

237 **sort** collection, assortment.

239–40 **Flatterers ... justice** those who flatter are hypocritical and will in their turn be treated hypocritically.

243 **Pluto** should be Plutus, the god of wealth.

245 **limping** i.e. slowly.

247 **post** swiftly.

scuttles quick movements.

248 **unvalu'd** undervalued.

249 **wanton humour** casual mood.

4 OFFICER   How scurvy proud he would look, when the
treasury was full. Well, let him go.

1 OFFICER   Yes, and the chippings of the butt'ry fly after   225
him, to scour his gold chain.

DUCHESS   Leave us. What do you think of these?

Exeunt OFFICERS

BOSOLA   That these are rogues, that in's prosperity,
But to have waited on his fortune, could have wish'd
His dirty stirrup riveted through their noses: 230
And follow'd after's mule, like a bear in a ring.
Would have prostituted their daughters to his lust;
Made their first born intelligencers; thought none happy
But such as were born under his bless'd planet;
And wore his livery: and do these lice drop off now?   235
Well, never look to have the like again;
He hath left a sort of flatt'ring rogues behind him,
Their doom must follow. Princes pay flatterers,
In their own money. Flatterers dissemble their vices,
And they dissemble their lies, that's justice.   240
Alas, poor gentleman, —

DUCHESS   Poor! he hath amply fill'd his coffers.

BOSOLA   Sure he was too honest. Pluto the god of
riches,
When he's sent, by Jupiter, to any man
He goes limping, to signify that wealth   245
That comes on God's name, comes slowly; but when
he's sent
On the devil's errand, he rides post, and comes in by
scuttles.
Let me show you what a most unvalu'd jewel
You have, in a wanton humour, thrown away,
To bless the man shall find him. He was an excellent   250
Courtier, and most faithful; a soldier, that thought it
As beastly to know his own value too little,

254 **virtue and form**   inward and outward qualities.

257 **whisp'ring room**   confession chamber.

258 **basely descended**   a commoner.

261 **want**   miss.

262 **know**   you should realise.

266 **Bermoothas**   Bermudas.

267 **politicians'**   those involved in plots and intrigues.

 bladders   i.e. filled with air, like balloons.

271 **Would needs ... thee**   caused your downfall.

282 **seminary**   seed bed, college for priests.

283 **unbenefic'd**   unsupported, unsalaried.

As devilish to acknowledge it too much;
Both his virtue and form deserv'd a far better fortune:
His discourse rather delighted to judge itself, than
 show itself.   255
His breast was fill'd with all perfection,
And yet it seem'd a private whisp'ring room:
It made so little noise of 't.
DUCHESS   But he was basely descended.
BOSOLA Will you make yourself a mercenary herald,
 Rather to examine men's pedigrees, than virtues? 260
 You shall want him:
 For know an honest statesman to a prince,
 Is like a cedar, planted by a spring,
 The spring bathes the tree's root, the grateful tree
 Rewards it with his shadow: you have not done so; 265
 I would sooner swim to the Bermoothas on
 Two politicians' rotten bladders, tied
 Together with an intelligencer's heart string
 Than depend on so changeable a prince's favour.
 Fare thee well, Antonio, since the malice of the world 270
 Would needs down with thee, it cannot be said yet
 That any ill happened unto thee,
 Considering thy fall was accomplished with virtue.
DUCHESS Oh, you render me excellent music.
BOSOLA   Say you?
DUCHESS This good one that you speak of, is my hus-
 band.   275
BOSOLA Do I not dream? Can this ambitious age
 Have so much goodness in't, as to prefer
 A man merely for worth: without these shadows
 Of wealth, and painted honours? possible?
DUCHESS I have had three children by him.
BOSOLA   Fortunate lady, 280
 For you have made your private nuptial bed
 The humble and fair seminary of peace.
 No question but many an unbenefic'd scholar

293 ***curious engine*** carefully made apparatus.

295 ***cabinets*** displays.

298 ***want coats*** run out of coats of arms.

307 ***Loretto*** a religious shrine; place of pilgrimage in central Italy where the Virgin Mary's house is said to have been carried by angels from Nazareth. (Our Lady of Loretto is the patron saint of aviators.)

311 ***train*** followers, household.

Shall pray for you, for this deed, and rejoice
That some preferment in the world can yet   285
Arise from merit. The virgins of your land,
That have no dowries, shall hope your example
Will raise them to rich husbands. Should you want
Soldiers, 'twould make the very Turks and Moors
Turn Christians, and serve you for this act.   290
Last, the neglected poets of your time,
In honour of this trophy of a man,
Rais'd by that curious engine, your white hand,
Shall thank you in your grave for't; and make that
More reverend than all the cabinets   295
Of living princes. For Antonio,
His fame shall likewise flow from many a pen,
When heralds shall want coats, to sell to men.

DUCHESS As I taste comfort, in this friendly speech,
So would I find concealment—

BOSOLA   Oh the secret of my prince,   300
Which I will wear on th'inside of my heart.

DUCHESS You shall take charge of all my coin, and
jewels,
And follow him, for he retires himself
To Ancona.

BOSOLA   So.

DUCHESS   Whither, within few days,
I mean to follow thee.

BOSOLA   Let me think: 305
I would wish your Grace to feign a pilgrimage
To Our Lady of Loretto, scarce seven leagues
From fair Ancona, so may you depart
Your country with more honour, and your flight
Will seem a princely progress, retaining   310
Your usual train about you.

DUCHESS   Sir, your direction
Shall lead me, by the hand.

321 *politician*   i.e. himself.

   quilted   quiet, secret.

324 *rests*   is left.

325 *quality*   profession.

327 *Prefers ... commendation*   promotes only greed or status.

328 *rais'd*   gain advancement.

329 **that paint weeds –**   are engaged in low occupations.

2 *that way*   i.e. as a soldier (before you were a cardinal).

3 *joins you in commission*   gives you joint command with.

CARIOLA   In my opinion,
  She were better progress to the baths at Lucca,
  Or go visit the Spa
  In Germany: for, if you will believe me,   315
  I do not like this jesting with religion,
  This feigned pilgrimage.
DUCHESS   Thou art a superstitious fool:
  Prepare us instantly for our departure.
  Past sorrows, let us moderately lament them,
  For those to come, seek wisely to prevent them.   320

                              Exit DUCHESS *with* CARIOLA

BOSOLA   A politician is the devil's quilted anvil,
  He fashions all sins on him, and the blows
  Are never heard; he may work in a lady's chamber,
  As here for proof. What rests, but I reveal
  All to my lord? Oh, this base quality   325
  Of intelligencer! Why, every quality i'th' world
  Prefers but gain, or commendation:
  Now for this act, I am certain to be rais'd,
  And men that paint weeds, to the life, are prais'd.

                                                         Exit

Scene three

(*Enter* CARDINAL, FERDINAND, MALATESTE, PESCARA, SILVIO,
DELIO)

CARDINAL   Must we turn soldier then?
MALATESTE   The Emperor,
  Hearing your worth that way, ere you attain'd
  This reverend garment, joins you in commission
  With the right fortunate soldier, the Marquis of Pes-
     cara
  And the famous Lannoy.

7 **plot**   plan, diagram.

10 **muster book**   register.

12 **gunpowder**   one of the components of gunpowder was used as a pain relief for toothache.

14 **leaguer**   camp.

17 **service**   campaigns.

20 **model**   drawings.

by the book   according to the textbook.

21 **almanac**   according to astrological forecasts.

22 **critical**   dangerous.

24 **taffeta**   light material used for scarves.

26 **taking**   being taken.

28 **pate**   head, skull.

29 **pot-gun**   loud-mouth.

30 **bore**   small hole.

31 **touch-hole**   where the flame was applied to light a charge to fire a cannon ball.

32 **sumpter-cloth**   ornamented saddle covering.

CARDINAL   He that had the honour   5
  Of taking the French king prisoner?
MALATESTE   The same.
  Here's a plot drawn for a new fortification
  At Naples.
FERDINAND   This great Count Malateste, I perceive
  Hath got employment.
DELIO   No employment, my lord,
  A marginal note in the muster book, that he is   10
  A voluntary lord.
FERDINAND   He's no soldier?
DELIO   He has worn gunpowder, in's hollow tooth,
  For the tooth-ache.
SILVIO   He comes to the leaguer with a full intent
  To eat fresh beef, and garlic; means to stay   15
  Till the scent be gone, and straight return to court.
DELIO   He hath read all the late service,
  As the City chronicle relates it,
  And keeps two painters going, only to express
  Battles in model.
SILVIO   Then he'll fight by the book.   20
DELIO   By the almanac, I think,
  To choose good days, and shun the critical.
  That's his mistress' scarf.
SILVIO   Yes, he protests
  He would do much for that taffeta, —
DELIO   I think he would run away from a battle   25
  To save it from taking prisoner.
SILVIO   He is horribly afraid
  Gunpowder will spoil the perfume on't, —
DELIO   I saw a Dutchman break his pate once
  For calling him pot-gun; he made his head
  Have a bore in't, like a musket.   30
SILVIO   I would he had made a touch-hole to't.
  He is indeed a guarded sumpter-cloth
  Only for the remove of the court.

37-9 **Foxes ... wrack for't**   reference to the Bible story (Judges 15) in which Samson tied pairs of foxes together, attached fire-brands to them and set them in the crops of the Philistines in order to destroy as much as possible.

40 **fantastical**   fanatical.

45 **shoeing-horn**   tool to ease on tight shoes.

46 **speculative**   thinking.

48 **salamander**   a mythical lizard-like creature which lived in fire.

50 **bad**   unhappy.

54 **lightens**   flashes.

55 **pangs of death**   omens of death, i.e. in the faces of the brothers.

59 **she**   the Duchess.

   riding hood   protection, cover.

60 **sun and tempest**   trouble, discovery.

(*Enter* BOSOLA)

PESCARA   Bosola arriv'd? What should be the business?
Some falling out amongst the cardinals.   35
These factions amongst great men, they are like
Foxes, when their heads are divided:
They carry fire in their tails, and all the country
About them goes to wrack for't.

SILVIO   What's that Bosola?

DELIO   I knew him in Padua, a fantastical scholar, like   40
such who study to know how many knots was in Hercules' club; of what colour Achilles' beard was, or
whether Hector were not troubled with the toothache.
He hath studied himself half blear-ey'd, to know the
true symmetry of Caesar's nose by a shoeing-horn: and   45
this he did to gain the name of a speculative man.

PESCARA   Mark Prince Ferdinand,
A very salamander lives in's eye,
To mock the eager violence of fire.

SILVIO   That cardinal hath made more bad faces with his   50
oppression than ever Michael Angelo made good ones:
he lifts up's nose, like a foul porpoise before a storm, —

PESCARA   The Lord Ferdinand laughs.

DELIO   Like a deadly cannon, that lightens ere it smokes.

PESCARA   These are your true pangs of death,   55
The pangs of life, that struggle with great statesmen, —

DELIO   In such a deformed silence, witches whisper their
charms.

CARDINAL   Doth she make religion her riding hood
To keep her from the sun and tempest?

FERDINAND   That: 60
That damns her. Methinks her fault and beauty
Blended together, show like leprosy,
The whiter, the fouler. I make it a question
Whether her beggarly brats were ever christ'ned.

65 *solicit*   request.

67 *your ceremony*   at which the Cardinal is taking on the role of soldier.

70 *honesty*   meant sarcastically.

s.d. **dumb-show**   mime.

CARDINAL   I will instantly solicit the state of Ancona   65
  To have them banish'd.
FERDINAND   You are for Loretto?
  I shall not be at your ceremony; fare you well:
  Write to the Duke of Malfi, my young nephew
  She had by her first husband, and acquaint him
  With's mother's honesty.
BOSOLA   I will.
FERDINAND   Antonio!   70
  A slave, that only smell'd of ink and counters,
  And nev'r in's life look'd like a gentleman,
  But in the audit time: go, go presently,
  Draw me out an hundred and fifty of our horse,
  And meet me at the fort-bridge.   75

Exeunt

Scene four

(*Enter* TWO PILGRIMS *to the Shrine of Our Lady of Loretto*)

1 PILGRIM   I have not seen a goodlier shrine than this,
  Yet I have visited many.
2 PILGRIM   The Cardinal of Aragon
  Is this day to resign his cardinal's hat;
  His sister duchess likewise is arriv'd
  To pay her vow of pilgrimage. I expect   5
  A noble ceremony.
1 PILGRIM   No question.— They come.

*Here the ceremony of the Cardinal's instalment in the habit of a soldier:
perform'd in delivering up his cross, hat, robes, and ring at the shrine;
and investing him with sword, helmet, shield, and spurs. Then* ANTONIO,
the DUCHESS *and their children, having presented themselves at the
shrine, are (by a form of banishment in dumb-show expressed towards
them by the* CARDINAL, *and the state of* ANCONA) *banished. During all*

121

28 **free prince**   independent ruler.
29 **free state**   an autonomous state but under the official protection of the
    Pope.
30 **forehearing**   hearing.
   looseness   immorality.
32 **dowager**   guardian for her son.

which ceremony this ditty is sung to very solemn music, by divers churchmen; and then

Exeunt

Arms and honours deck thy story,
To thy fame's eternal glory,
Adverse fortune ever fly thee,   The Author
No disastrous fate come nigh thee.   disclaims this   10
                           Ditty to be his.
I alone will sing thy praises,
Whom to honour virtue raises;
And thy study that divine is,
Bent to martial discipline is:
Lay aside all those robes lie by thee,   15
Crown thy arts with arms: they'll beautify thee.

O worthy of worthiest name, adorn'd in this manner,
Lead bravely thy forces on, under war's warlike banner:
O mayst thou prove fortunate in all martial courses,
Guide thou still by skill, in arts and forces: 20
Victory attend thee nigh, whilst fame sings loud thy powers,
Triumphant conquest crown thy head, and blessings pour down
    showers.

1 PILGRIM   Here's a strange turn of state: who would
    have thought
So great a lady would have match'd herself
Unto so mean a person? Yet the Cardinal   25
Bears himself much too cruel.
2 PILGRIM   They are banish'd
1 PILGRIM   But I would ask what power hath this state
Of Ancona, to determine of a free prince?
2 PILGRIM   They are a free state sir, and her brother
    show'd
How that the Pope, forehearing of her looseness,   30
Hath seiz'd into th' protection of the Church
The dukedom which she held as dowager.

1 **Banish'd Ancona?** banished from Ancona?

2 **train** followers.

5 **buntings** small birds.

9 **Right** just.

10–11 **From decay'd ... sinks** nobody knows you when you're down and out.

1 PILGRIM But by what justice?
2 PILGRIM   Sure I think by none,
    Only her brother's instigation.
1 PILGRIM What was it, with such violence he took   35
    Off from her finger?
2 PILGRIM   'Twas her wedding-ring,
    Which he vow'd shortly he would sacrifice
    To his revenge.
1 PILGRIM   Alas Antonio!
    If that a man be thrust into a well,
    No matter who sets hand to't, his own weight   40
    Will bring him sooner to th' bottom. Come, let's
      hence.
    Fortune makes this conclusion general,
    All things do help th'unhappy man to fall.

                                      Exeunt

Scene five

(*Enter* ANTONIO, DUCHESS, CHILDREN, CARIOLA, SERVANTS)

DUCHESS Banish'd Ancona?
ANTONIO   Yes, you see what power
    Lightens in great men's breath.
DUCHESS   Is all our train
    Shrunk to this poor remainder?
ANTONIO   These poor men,
    Which have got little in your service, vow
    To take your fortune. But your wiser buntings   5
    Now they are fledg'd are gone.
DUCHESS   They have done wisely;
    This puts me in mind of death: physicians thus,
    With their hands full of money, use to give o'er
    Their patients.
ANTONIO   Right the fashion of the world:
    From decay'd fortunes every flatterer shrinks,   10

20 **carol**   sing.

21 **happily o'ertane**   fortunately overtaken.

23 **blanch**   whiten.

28 **politic equivocation**   double use of words to hide the truth.

31 **strew'd**   covered.

Men cease to build where the foundation sinks.

DUCHESS   I had a very strange dream tonight.

ANTONIO   What was't?

DUCHESS   Methought I wore my coronet of state,
And on a sudden all the diamonds
Were chang'd to pearls.

ANTONIO   My interpretation   15
Is, you'll weep shortly; for to me, the pearls
Do signify your tears.

DUCHESS   The birds, that live i'th' field
On the wild benefit of nature, live
Happier than we; for they may choose their mates,
And carol their sweet pleasures to the spring.   20

(*Enter* BOSOLA *with a letter which he presents to the* DUCHESS)

BOSOLA   You are happily o'ertane.

DUCHESS   From my brother?

BOSOLA   Yes, from the Lord Ferdinand; your brother,
All love, and safety —

DUCHESS   Thou dost blanch mischief;
Wouldst make it white. See, see; like to calm weather
At sea before a tempest, false hearts speak fair   25
To those they intend most mischief. (*she reads*) *A Letter:
Send* Antonio *to me; I want his head in a business.*
(A politic equivocation)
He doth not want your counsel, but your head;
That is, he cannot sleep till you be dead.   30
And here's another pitfall, that's strew'd o'er
With roses: mark it, 'tis a cunning one:
*I stand engaged for your husband for several debts at Naples:
let not that trouble him, I had rather have his heart than his
money.*   35
And I believe so too.

BOSOLA   What do you believe?

DUCHESS   That he so much distrusts my husband's love,
He will by no means believe his heart is with him

40 *circumvent* trap.

41 *league* alliance.

43 *politic* manoeuvring, manipulative.

48 *abroad* everywhere.

53 *adamant* magnet.

55 *conjure* beseech, beg.

57–8 **Let us not ... bottom** let us not entrust all we have left in one unsure boat.

61 *curious* skilled.

in sunder apart.

Until he see it. The devil is not cunning enough
To circumvent us in riddles.   40
BOSOLA   Will you reject that noble and free league
Of amity and love which I present you?
DUCHESS   Their league is like that of some politic kings
Only to make themselves of strength and power
To be our after-ruin: tell them so.   45
BOSOLA   And what from you?
ANTONIO   Thus tell them: I will not come.
BOSOLA   And what of this?
ANTONIO   My brothers have dispers'd
Bloodhounds abroad; which till I hear are muzzl'd
No truce, though hatch'd with ne'er such politic skill
Is safe, that hangs upon our enemies' will.   50
I'll not come at them.
BOSOLA   This proclaims your breeding.
Every small thing draws a base mind to fear;
As the adamant draws iron: fare you well sir,
You shall shortly hear from's.

                                                    Exit

DUCHESS   I suspect some ambush:
Therefore by all my love I do conjure you   55
To take your eldest son, and fly towards Milan;
Let us not venture all this poor remainder
In one unlucky bottom.
ANTONIO   You counsel safely.
Best of my life, farewell. Since we must part
Heaven hath a hand in't: but no otherwise   60
Than as some curious artist takes in sunder
A clock, or watch, when it is out of frame
To bring't in better order.
DUCHESS   I know not which is best,
To see you dead, or part with you. Farewell boy,
Thou art happy, that thou hast not understanding   65
To know thy misery. For all our wit

                                                    129

68 **eternal Church**   eternal life, after death.

72 **cassia**   fragrant bark giving off scent when crushed.

76 **scourge ... top**   whip his spinning top.

78 **scourge-stick**   whip for a top.

89 **sound**   measure the extent or depth of.

90 **laurel**   symbol of success.

s.d **vizarded**   masked or with helmets on and visors down.

93 **over-charg'd**   overburdened, weighed down.

And reading brings us to a truer sense
Of sorrow. In the eternal Church, sir,
I do hope we shall not part thus.
ANTONIO   O be of comfort,
   Make patience a noble fortitude: 70
   And think not how unkindly we are us'd.
   Man, like to cassia, is prov'd best being bruis'd.
DUCHESS   Must I like to a slave-born Russian,
   Account it praise to suffer tyranny?
   And yet, O Heaven, thy heavy hand is in't.   75
   I have seen my little boy oft scourge his top,
   And compar'd myself to't: nought made me e'er go right,
   But Heaven's scourge-stick.
ANTONIO   Do not weep:
   Heaven fashion'd us of nothing; and we strive
   To bring ourselves to nothing. Farewell Cariola,   80
   And thy sweet armful. (*to the* DUCHESS) If I do never see
     thee more,
   Be a good mother to your little ones,
   And save them from the tiger: fare you well.
DUCHESS   Let me look upon you once more: for that
     speech
   Came from a dying father: your kiss is colder   85
   Than I have seen an holy anchorite
   Give to a dead man's skull.
ANTONIO   My heart is turn'd to a heavy lump of lead,
   With which I sound my danger: fare you well.

                            Exit (with elder SON)

DUCHESS   My laurel is all withered.   90
CARIOLA   Look, Madam, what a troop of armed men
   Make toward us.

(*Enter* BOSOLA *with a guard, vizarded*)

DUCHESS   O, they are very welcome:
   When Fortune's wheel is over-charg'd with princes,

95 **sudden**   swift.

    adventure   prey.

97 **that counterfeits ... thunder**   only God should put asunder those who are married.

105 **Charon's boat**   in classical mythology, he ferried the dead across the river Styx to the underworld.

112 **prattle**   talk, chatter.

116 **low fellow**   referring to her husband.

117 **that counterfeit ... other**   your mask into your face.

118 **of no birth**   a commoner.

The weight makes it move swift. I would have my ruin
Be sudden. I am your adventure, am I not?   95
BOSOLA   You are: you must see your husband no more,—
DUCHESS   What devil art thou, that counterfeits Heaven's
   thunder?
BOSOLA   Is that terrible? I would have you tell me whether
   Is that note worse that frights the silly birds
   Out of the corn; or that which doth allure them   100
   To the nets? You have heark'ned to the last too much.
DUCHESS   O misery! like to a rusty o'ercharg'd cannon,
   Shall I never fly in pieces? Come: to what prison?
BOSOLA   To none.
DUCHESS   Whither then?
BOSOLA   To your palace.
DUCHESS   I have heard that Charon's boat serves to con-
   vey   105
   All o'er the dismal lake, but brings none back again.
BOSOLA   Your brothers mean you safety and pity.
DUCHESS   Pity!
   With such a pity men preserve alive
   Pheasants and quails, when they are not fat enough   110
   To be eaten.
BOSOLA   These are your children?
DUCHESS   Yes.
BOSOLA   Can they prattle?
DUCHESS   No:
   But I intend, since they were born accurs'd;
   Curses shall be their first language.
BOSOLA   Fie, Madam!   115
   Forget this base, low fellow.
DUCHESS   Were I a man,
   I'll'd beat that counterfeit face into thy other—
BOSOLA   One of no birth.
DUCHESS   Say that he was born mean,
   Man is most happy, when's own actions
   Be arguments and examples of his virtue.   120

133

125 **Dog-fish** fish of the shark family.
127 **high state of floods** our high society of the sea.
131 **Smelts and Shrimps** small fry.
132 **Dog-ship** as in 'Your Lordship'.
    reverence a bow or curtsey.
142 **sways** power.

BOSOLA   A barren, beggarly virtue.
DUCHESS   I prithee, who is greatest, can you tell?
  Sad tales befit my woe: I'll tell you one.
  A Salmon, as she swam unto the sea,
  Met with a Dog-fish; who encounters her   125
  With this rough language: 'Why art thou so bold
  To mix thyself with our high state of floods
  Being no eminent courtier, but one
  That for the calmest and fresh time o'th' year
  Dost live in shallow rivers, rank'st thyself   130
  With silly Smelts and Shrimps? And darest thou
  Pass by our Dog-ship without reverence?'
  'O', quoth the Salmon, 'sister, be at peace:
  Thank Jupiter, we both have pass'd the Net,
  Our value never can be truly known,   135
  Till in the Fisher's basket we be shown;
  I'th' Market then my price may be the higher,
  Even when I am nearest to the Cook, and fire.'
  So, to great men, the moral may be stretched.
  Men oft are valued high, when th'are most wretch'd.   140
  But come: whither you please. I am arm'd 'gainst mis-
    ery:
  Bent to all sways of the oppressor's will.
  There's no deep valley, but near some great hill.

                                      Exeunt

12 **disdain** contempt.

13 **mastives** mastiff dogs.

   tying being tied up.

14 **apprehend** be aware of.

Act Four

Scene one

(*Enter* FERDINAND *and* BOSOLA)

FERDINAND   How doth our sister Duchess bear herself
  In her imprisonment?
BOSOLA   Nobly: I'll describe her:
  She's sad, as one long us'd to't: and she seems
  Rather to welcome the end of misery
  Than shun it: a behaviour so noble,   5
  As gives a majesty to adversity:
  You may discern the shape of loveliness
  More perfect in her tears, than in her smiles;
  She will muse four hours together: and her silence,
  Methinks, expresseth more than if she spake.   10
FERDINAND   Her melancholy seems to be fortifi'd
  With a strange disdain.
BOSOLA   'Tis so: and this restraint
  (Like English mastives, that grow fierce with tying)
  Makes her too passionately apprehend
  Those pleasures she's kept from.
FERDINAND   Curse upon her!   15
  I will no longer study in the book
  Of another's heart: inform her what I told you.

                                       Exit

(*Enter* DUCHESS, CARIOLA *and* SERVANTS)

BOSOLA   All comfort to your Grace; —
DUCHESS   I will have none.
  'Pray-thee, why dost thou wrap thy poison'd pills
  In gold and sugar?   20

137

27 *reconcile*   restore friendship.
39 *sacrament*   marriage.
41 *liv'd thus*   i.e. in darkness.
42 *i'th' light*   in public.

BOSOLA   Your elder brother the Lord Ferdinand
  Is come to visit you: and sends you word,
  'Cause once he rashly made a solemn vow
  Never to see you more, he comes i'th' night;
  And prays you, gently, neither torch nor taper   25
  Shine in your chamber: he will kiss your hand;
  And reconcile himself: but, for his vow,
  He dares not see you.
DUCHESS   At his pleasure.
  Take hence the lights: he's come.

        (*Exeunt* SERVANTS *with lights*; *enter* FERDINAND)

FERDINAND   Where are you?
DUCHESS   Here sir.
FERDINAND   This darkness suits you well.
DUCHESS   I would ask your pardon.   30
FERDINAND   You have it;
  For I account it the honorabl'st revenge
  Where I may kill, to pardon: where are your cubs?
DUCHESS   Whom?
FERDINAND   Call them your children;   35
  For though our national law distinguish bastards
  From true legitimate issue, compassionate nature
  Makes them all equal.
DUCHESS   Do you visit me for this?
  You violate a sacrament o'th' Church
  Shall make you howl in hell for't.
FERDINAND   It had been well.   40
  Could you have liv'd thus always: for indeed
  You were too much i'th' light. But no more;
  I come to seal my peace with you: here's a hand,

(*gives her a dead man's hand*)

  To which you have vow'd much love: the ring upon't
  You gave.
DUCHESS   I affectionately kiss it.   45

50 **ow'd** owned.

s.d. **traverse** small space at the back of the stage.

56 **piece** body.

62 **wastes** harms, affects.

65 **yond's** yonder is, there is.

FERDINAND   Pray do: and bury the print of it in your
    heart.
  I will leave this ring with you, for a love-token:
  And the hand, as sure as the ring: and do not doubt
  But you shall have the heart too. When you need a
    friend
  Send it to him that ow'd it: you shall see   50
  Whether he can aid you.
DUCHESS   You are very cold.
  I fear you are not well after your travel:
  Ha! Lights: Oh horrible!
FERDINAND   Let her have lights enough.

Exit

(*Enter* SERVANTS *with lights*)

DUCHESS   What witchcraft doth he practise, that he hath
    left
  A dead man's hand here? —   55

Here is discover'd, behind a traverse, the artificial figures of ANTONIO
and his children; appearing as if they were dead.

BOSOLA   Look you: here's the piece from which 'twas
    tane;
  He doth present you this sad spectacle,
  That now you know directly they are dead,
  Hereafter you may, wisely, cease to grieve
  For that which cannot be recovered.   60
DUCHESS   There is not between heaven and earth one
    wish
  I stay for after this: it wastes me more,
  Than were't my picture, fashion'd out of wax,
  Stuck with a magical needle, and then buried
  In some foul dunghill: and yond's an excellent property 65
  For a tyrant, which I would account mercy, —
BOSOLA   What's that?

72 **Portia** Brutus's wife, who committed suicide after her husband's death by swallowing hot coals.

75 **enjoins** recommends, requires.

80 **broke upon the wheel** to break the bones of a victim on a specially designed wheel was a common form of official torture.

82 **dispatch** kill.

90 **vipers** the sense of this is unclear but the word would seem to represent torments; (some editions have vapours).

DUCHESS   If they would bind me to that lifeless trunk,
   And let me freeze to death.
BOSOLA   Come, you must live.
DUCHESS   That's the greatest torture souls feel in hell,   70
   In hell: that they must live, and cannot die.
   Portia, I'll new kindle thy coals again,
   And revive the rare and almost dead example
   Of a loving wife.
BOSOLA   O fie! despair? remember
   You are a Christian.
DUCHESS   The Church enjoins fasting: 75
   I'll starve myself to death.
BOSOLA   Leave this vain sorrow;
   Things being at the worst, begin to mend:
   The bee when he hath shot his sting into your hand
   May then play with your eyelid.
DUCHESS   Good comfortable fellow
   Persuade a wretch that's broke upon the wheel   80
   To have all his bones new set: entreat him live,
   To be executed again. Who must dispatch me?
   I account this world a tedious theatre,
   For I do play a part in't 'gainst my will.
BOSOLA   Come, be of comfort, I will save your life.   85
DUCHESS   Indeed I have not leisure to tend so small a
   business.
BOSOLA   Now, by my life, I pity you.
DUCHESS   Thou art a fool then,
   To waste thy pity on a thing so wretch'd
   As cannot pity itself. I am full of daggers.
   Puff! let me blow these vipers from me.   90

(*Enter* SERVANT)

   What are you?
SERVANT   One that wishes you long life.
DUCHESS   I would thou wert hang'd for the horrible
   curse

93 **grow** become.

94 **miracles of pity** religious images for the purpose of making one feel pity.

97 **three smiling seasons** spring, summer, autumn.

98 **Russian winter** lasting the whole year.

101 **lanes** inroads.

104 **mortified** sanctified through suffering.

110 **plagu'd in art** made to suffer through artifice, trickery.

112 **quality** craft.

Thou hast given me: I shall shortly grow one
Of the miracles of pity. I'll go pray. No,
I'll go curse.

BOSOLA   Oh fie!

DUCHESS   I could curse the stars.   95

BOSOLA Oh fearful!

DUCHESS And those three smiling seasons of the year
Into a Russian winter: nay the world
To its first chaos.

BOSOLA Look you, the stars shine still.

DUCHESS   Oh, but you must
Remember, my curse hath a great way to go: 100
Plagues, that make lanes through largest families,
Consume them.

BOSOLA   Fie lady!

DUCHESS   Let them like tyrants
Never be rememb'red, but for the ill they have done:
Let all the zealous prayers of mortified
Churchmen forget them, —

BOSOLA   O uncharitable!   105

DUCHESS Let Heaven, a little while, cease crowning
    martyrs
To punish them.
Go, howl them this: and say I long to bleed.
It is some mercy when men kill with speed.

Exit (with SERVANTS)

(*Enter* FERDINAND)

FERDINAND Excellent; as I would wish: she's plagu'd in
    art.   110
These presentations are but fram'd in wax
By the curious master in that quality,
Vincentio Lauriola, and she takes them
For true substantial bodies.

145

117 **penitential garment**   white garment worn by women guilty of adultery who were then paraded publicly.

119 **beads**   rosary beads.

120 **my blood**   his family blood. Note: he is her twin.

122 **masques**   a form of dramatic spectacle involving music, dance and acting.

   courtesans   prostitutes.

125 **forth**   from.

132 **intelligence**   role as spy.

133 **last cruel lie**   the deception of the wax images.

135 **nothing of kin**   unfamiliar.

139 **Intemperate**   unharmonious, unbalanced (i.e. the bodily humours are out of balance) and desperate situations require desperate remedies.

BOSOLA   Why do you do this?

FERDINAND   To bring her to despair.

BOSOLA   'Faith, end here;   115
And go no farther in your cruelty,
Send her a penitential garment, to put on
Next to her delicate skin, and furnish her
With beads and prayerbooks.

FERDINAND   Damn her! that body of hers,
While that my blood ran pure in't, was more worth   120
Than that which thou wouldst comfort, call'd a soul.
I will send her masques of common courtesans,
Have her meat serv'd up by bawds and ruffians,
And, 'cause she'll needs be mad, I am resolv'd
To remove forth the common hospital   125
All the mad folk, and place them near her lodging:
There let them practise together, sing, and dance,
And act their gambols to the full o'th' moon:
If she can sleep the better for it, let her.
Your work is almost ended.

BOSOLA   Must I see her again?   130

FERDINAND   Yes.

BOSOLA   Never.

FERDINAND   You must.

BOSOLA   Never in mine own shape;
That's forfeited by my intelligence,
And this last cruel lie: when you send me next,
The business shall be comfort.

FERDINAND   Very likely:
Thy pity is nothing of kin to thee. Antonio   135
Lurks about Milan; thou shalt shortly thither,
To feed a fire as great as my revenge,
Which nev'r will slack, till it have spent his fuel;
Intemperate agues make physicians cruel.

                                        Exeunt

1 *consort* collection of musicians.
12 *durance* weight, imprisonment.
17 *muse* meditate.

Scene two

(*Enter* DUCHESS *and* CARIOLA)

DUCHESS   What hideous noise was that?
CARIOLA   'Tis the wild consort
  Of madmen, lady, which your tyrant brother
  Hath plac'd about your lodging. This tyranny,
  I think, was never practis'd till this hour.
DUCHESS   Indeed I thank him: nothing but noise, and
    folly   5
  Can keep me in my right wits, whereas reason
  And silence make me stark mad. Sit down,
  Discourse to me some dismal tragedy.
CARIOLA   O 'twill increase your melancholy.
DUCHESS   Thou art deceiv'd;
  To hear of greater grief would lessen mine.   10
  This is a prison?
CARIOLA   Yes, but you shall live
  To shake this durance off.
DUCHESS   Thou art a fool:
  The robin red-breast and the nightingale
  Never live long in cages.
CARIOLA   Pray dry your eyes.
  What think you of Madam?   15
DUCHESS   Of nothing:
  When I muse thus, I sleep.
CARIOLA   Like a madman, with your eyes open?
DUCHESS   Dost thou think we shall know one another
  In th'other world?
CARIOLA   Yes, out of question.   20
DUCHESS   O that it were possible we might
  But hold some two days' conference with the dead,
  From them I should learn somewhat, I am sure

29 **tann'd**   both sunburned and whipped.

31 **custom**   frequency, habit.

34 **reverend**   revered, respected.

36 **Fortune ... eyesight**   Fortune, like Justice, is often depicted as blindfolded; here, if Fortune can see at all, it is merely to look on at the Duchess's misfortune and do nothing.

44 **imposthume**   boil, abscess – in this anecdote, a mental not physical ailment.

46 **secular**   not monastic.

50 **failing of't**   when it didn't happen.

52 **usher**   servant.

I never shall know here. I'll tell thee a miracle,
I am not mad yet, to my cause of sorrow.   25
Th'heaven o'er my head seems made of molten brass,
The earth of flaming sulphur, yet I am not mad.
I am acquainted with sad misery,
As the tann'd galley-slave is with his oar.
Necessity makes me suffer constantly.   30
And custom makes it easy. Who do I look like now?
CARIOLA   Like to your picture in the gallery,
A deal of life in show, but none in practice:
Or rather like some reverend monument
Whose ruins are even pitied.
DUCHESS   Very proper: 35
And Fortune seems only to have her eyesight,
To behold my tragedy.
How now! what noise is that?

(*Enter* SERVANT)

SERVANT   I am come to tell you,
Your brother hath intended you some sport.
A great physician when the Pope was sick   40
Of a deep melancholy, presented him
With several sorts of madmen, which wild object,
Being full of change and sport, forc'd him to laugh,
And so th'imposthume broke: the selfsame cure
The Duke intends on you.
DUCHESS   Let them come in.   45
SERVANT   There's a mad lawyer, and a secular priest,
A doctor that hath forfeited his wits
By jealousy; an astrologian,
That in his works said such a day o'th' month
Should be the day of doom; and, failing of't,   50
Ran mad; an English tailor, craz'd i'th' brain
With the study of new fashion; a gentleman usher

54 *salutations* greetings.

57 *hind'red transportation* prevented from transporting, exporting.

58 *broker* dealer.

67 **bell** bellow.

68 **yerksome** irksome.

69 **corrosiv'd** corroded.

70 **quire** choir.

72 **sing like swans** as in swan-song, final most beautiful, song.

75 *glass* magnifying glass.

82 *tithe* see note to Act 2, scene 1, line 113.

Quite beside himself with care to keep in mind
The number of his lady's salutations,
Or 'How do you?' she employ'd him in each
    morning: 55
A farmer too, an excellent knave in grain,
Mad, 'cause he was hind'red transportation;
And let one broker, that's mad, loose to these,
You'ld think the devil were among them.

DUCHESS   Sit Cariola: let them loose when you please,   60
For I am chain'd to endure all your tyranny.

(*Enter* MADMEN)

Here, by a madman, this song is sung to a dismal kind of music.

> *O let us howl, some heavy note,*
>   *some deadly-dogged howl,*
> *Sounding, as from the threat'ning throat,*
>   *of beasts, and fatal fowl.*   65
> *As ravens, screech-owls, bulls, and bears,*
>   *We'll bell, and bawl our parts,*
> *Till yerksome noise, have cloy'd your ears,*
>   *and corrosiv'd your hearts.*
> *At last when as our quire wants breath,*   70
>   *our bodies being blest,*
> *We'll sing like swans, to welcome death,*
>   *and die in love and rest.*

MAD ASTROLOGER   Doomsday not come yet? I'll draw it
nearer by a perspective, or make a glass, that shall set   75
all the world on fire upon an instant. I cannot sleep,
my pillow is stufft with a litter of porcupines.

MAD LAWYER   Hell is a mere glass-house, where the devils are continually blowing up women's souls on hollow irons, and the fire never goes out.   80

MAD PRIEST   I will lie with every woman in my parish
the tenth night: I will tithe them over like haycocks.

153

83 **pothecary** apothecary, preparer of medicines.

   outgo outdo.

85 **allum** alum, mineral containing aluminium and potassium with astringent properties.

86 **over-straining** ranting, zealous preaching.

89–90 **woodcock** simple person.

92–3 **Greek ... translation** refers to different translations of the Bible, the speaker only trusting the Swiss (Geneva) version; this is a parody of Puritan priests.

94 **lay** explain.

96 **corrosive** a sharp medicine.

103–4 **rope-maker** hangman, or associate of one.

106–7 **wench's placket** woman's skirt a, 'placket' being a skirt opening.

108 **caroche** coach.

115 **possets** drinks to assist sleep.

117 **made a soap-boiler costive** made a worker engaged in making soap constipated. (Apparently it was a trade likely to encourage diarrhoea.)

MAD DOCTOR Shall my pothecary outgo me, because I
am a cuckold? I have found out his roguery: he makes
allum of his wife's urine, and sells it to Puritans, that   85
have sore throats with over-straining.

MAD ASTROLOGER I have skill in heraldry.

MAD LAWYER Hast?

MAD ASTROLOGER You do give for your crest a woodcock's head, with the brains pick'd out on't. You are a   90
very ancient gentleman.

MAD PRIEST Greek is turn'd Turk; we are only to be
sav'd by the Helvetian translation.

MAD ASTROLOGER (*to* LAWYER) Come on sir, I will lay
the law to you.   95

MAD LAWYER Oh, rather lay a corrosive, the law will eat
to the bone.

MAD PRIEST He that drinks but to satisfy nature is
damn'd.

MAD DOCTOR If I had my glass here, I would show a   100
sight should make all the women here call me mad
doctor.

MAD ASTROLOGER (*pointing to* PRIEST) What's he, a rope-
maker?

MAD LAWYER No, no, no, a snuffling knave, that while   105
he shows the tombs, will have his hand in a wench's
placket.

MAD PRIEST Woe to the caroche that brought home my
wife from the masque, at three o'clock in the morning;
it had a large feather bed in it.   110

MAD DOCTOR I have pared the devil's nails forty times,
roasted them in raven's eggs, and cur'd agues with
them.

MAD PRIEST Get me three hundred milch bats, to make
possets to procure sleep.   115

MAD DOCTOR All the college may throw their caps at me,
I have made a soap-boiler costive: it was my master-
piece: —

155

s.d. **music answerable thereunto**   with suitable music.

124 *insensible*   not realised.

128 *box of worm seed*   the body is a container which is good only for breeding worms.

129 *salvatory*   ointment box.

green   not yet ready.

mummy   medicine made from mummified bodies.

130 *cruded*   curdled.

puff-paste   puff pastry, light and insubstantial.

137 *compass*   boundaries.

139 *riot*   signs of age.

143–4 *breeds its teeth*   is teething.

*Here the dance consisting of 8 madmen, with music answerable thereunto,
after which* BOSOLA, *like an old man, enters.*

DUCHESS   Is he mad too?

SERVANT   Pray question him; I'll leave you.

                              Exeunt SERVANT *and* MADMEN

BOSOLA   I am come to make thy tomb.

DUCHESS   Ha! my tomb?   120
  Thou speak'st as if I lay upon my death-bed,
  Gasping for breath: dost thou perceive me sick?

BOSOLA   Yes, and the more dangerously, since thy sick-
  ness is insensible.

DUCHESS   Thou art not mad, sure; dost know me?   125

BOSOLA   Yes.

DUCHESS   Who am I?

BOSOLA   Thou art a box of worm seed, at best, but a
  salvatory of green mummy: what's this flesh? a little
  cruded milk, fantastical puff-paste: our bodies are   130
  weaker than those paper prisons boys use to keep flies
  in: more contemptible; since ours is to preserve earth-
  worms: didst thou ever see a lark in a cage? such is the
  soul in the body: this world is like her little turf of
  grass, and the heaven o'er our heads, like her looking-   135
  glass, only gives us a miserable knowledge of the small
  compass of our prison.

DUCHESS   Am not I thy Duchess?

BOSOLA   Thou art some great woman, sure; for riot begins to sit on thy forehead (clad in grey hairs) twenty   140
  years sooner than on a merry milkmaid's. Thou
  sleep'st worse, than if a mouse should be forc'd to take
  up her lodging in a cat's ear: a little infant, that breeds
  its teeth, should it lie with thee, would cry out, as if
  thou wert the more unquiet bedfellow.   145

DUCHESS   I am Duchess of Malfi still.

148 **Glories**   great deeds, fame.

158 *fantastical*   fanciful.

160–66 *Princes' images ... their faces*   effigies of great men on their tombs are made in all sorts of positions, not just in the traditional one of prayer.

169 *charnel*   store for human bones.

173–4 *I have so much ... good*   the Duchess offers her own blood to her brothers, perhaps with an implication of 'much good may it do them'.

175 *presence chamber*   normally, the stately and formal room in which a prince received visitors.

BOSOLA   That makes thy sleeps so broken:
  Glories, like glow-worms, afar off shine bright,
  But look'd to near, have neither heat nor light.
DUCHESS   Thou art very plain.   150
BOSOLA   My trade is to flatter the dead, not the living;
  I am a tomb-maker.
DUCHESS   And thou com'st to make my tomb?
BOSOLA   Yes.
DUCHESS   Let me be a little merry;   155
  Of what stuff wilt thou make it?
BOSOLA   Nay, resolve me first, of what fashion?
DUCHESS   Why, do we grow fantastical in our death-bed?
  Do we affect fashion in the grave?
BOSOLA   Most ambitiously. Princes' images on their
  tombs   160
  Do not lie as they were wont, seeming to pray
  Up to Heaven: but with their hands under their
  cheeks,
  As if they died of the tooth-ache; they are not carved
  With their eyes fix'd upon the stars; but as
  Their minds were wholly bent upon the world,   165
  The self-same way they seem to turn their faces.
DUCHESS   Let me know fully therefore the effect
  Of this thy dismal preparation,
  This talk, fit for a charnel.
BOSOLA   Now I shall;

(*Enter* EXECUTIONERS *with a coffin, cords, and a bell*)

  Here is a present from your princely brothers,   170
  And may it arrive welcome, for it brings
  Last benefit, last sorrow.
DUCHESS   Let me see it.
  I have so much obedience, in my blood,
  I wish it in their veins, to do them good.
BOSOLA   This is your last presence chamber.   175
CARIOLA   O my sweet lady!

181 *mortification*   readiness for death.

183 **whistler**   bird whose cry was considered ominous.

187 **competent**   sufficient.

191–3 **Sin ... of terror**   sin is part of man's make-up at conception and exerts an influence throughout life.

194 **Strew ... sweet**   ornament your hair; a bridal ritual.

DUCHESS   Peace; it affrights not me.
BOSOLA   I am the common bellman,
  That usually is sent to condemn'd persons,
  The night before they suffer.
DUCHESS   Even now thou said'st
  Thou wast a tomb-maker?
BOSOLA   'Twas to bring you   180
  By degrees to mortification. Listen:

(*rings the bell*)

> *Hark, now every thing is still,*
> *The screech-owl and the whistler shrill*
> *Call upon our Dame, aloud,*
> *And bid her quickly don her shroud.*   185
> *Much you had of land and rent,*
> *Your length in clay's now competent.*
> *A long war disturb'd your mind,*
> *Here your perfect peace is sign'd.*
> *Of what is't fools make such vain keeping?*   190
> *Sin their conception, their birth, weeping:*
> *Their life, a general mist of error,*
> *Their death, a hideous storm of terror.*
> *Strew your hair with powders sweet:*
> *Don clean linen, bath your feet,*   195
> *And, the foul fiend more to check,*
> *A crucifix let bless your neck.*
> *'Tis now full tide 'tween night and day,*
> *End your groan, and come away.*

(EXECUTIONERS *approach*)

CARIOLA   Hence villains, tyrants, murderers. Alas!   200
  What will you do with my lady? Call for help.
DUCHESS   To whom, to our next neighbours? They are
    mad-folks.
BOSOLA   Remove that noise.

(EXECUTIONERS *seize* CARIOLA, *who struggles.*)

206 **reversion** inheritance.

212 **apoplexy** brain haemorrhage.

catarrh not the modern meaning but, again, a brain haemorrhage.

221 **cassia** perfume.

222 **several** different.

225 **both ways** presumably, death can come for you – or you can seek it.

229 **would fain** wish to.

woman's fault supposedly, talking too much.

DUCHESS   Farewell Cariola,
  In my last will I have not much to give;
  A many hungry guests have fed upon me,   205
  Thine will be a poor reversion.
CARIOLA   I will die with her.
DUCHESS I pray thee look thou giv'st my little boy
  Some syrup for his cold, and let the girl
  Say her prayers, ere she sleep.

(CARIOLA *is forced off.*)

                           Now what you please,
  What death?
BOSOLA   Strangling: here are your executioners.   210
DUCHESS I forgive them:
  The apoplexy, catarrh, or cough o'th' lungs
  Would do as much as they do.
BOSOLA Doth not death fright you?
DUCHESS   Who would be afraid on't?
  Knowing to meet such excellent company   215
  In th'other world.
BOSOLA   Yet, methinks,
  The manner of your death should much afflict you,
  This cord should terrify you?
DUCHESS   Not a whit:
  What would it pleasure me, to have my throat cut
  With diamonds? or to be smothered   220
  With cassia? or to be shot to death, with pearls?
  I know death hath ten thousand several doors
  For men to take their *Exits*: and 'tis found
  They go on such strange geometrical hinges,
  You may open them both ways: any way, for Heaven
     sake,   225
  So I were out of your whispering. Tell my brothers
  That I perceive death, now I am well awake,
  Best gift is, they can give, or I can take.
  I would fain put off my last woman's fault,
  I'll'd not be tedious to you.

238 *mandragora*   mandrake, a plant bestowing sleep.
249 *kept her counsel*   kept her secrets.

EXECUTIONERS   We are ready.   230
DUCHESS Dispose my breath how please you, but my
    body
  Bestow upon my women, will you?
EXECUTIONERS   Yes.
DUCHESS Pull, and pull strongly, for your able strength
  Must pull down heaven upon me;
  Yet stay, heaven gates are not so highly arch'd   235
  As princes' palaces: they that enter there
  Must go upon their knees. Come violent death,
  Serve for mandragora to make me sleep;
  Go tell my brothers, when I am laid out,
  They then may feed in quiet.

They strangle her.

BOSOLA   Where's the waiting woman? 240
  Fetch her. Some other strangle the children.

      (*Exeunt* EXECUTIONERS. *Enter one with* CARIOLA)

  Look you, there sleeps your mistress.
CARIOLA   O you are damn'd
  Perpetually for this. My turn is next,
  Is't not so ordered?
BOSOLA   Yes, and I am glad
  You are so well prepar'd for't.
CARIOLA   You are deceiv'd sir,   245
  I am not prepar'd for't. I will not die,
  I will first come to my answer; and know
  How I have offended.
BOSOLA   Come, dispatch her.
  You kept her counsel, now you shall keep ours.
CARIOLA I will not die, I must not, I am contracted
  To a young gentleman.   250
EXECUTIONER (*showing the noose*) Here's your wedding-
  ring.

252 *discover* reveal, make known.
256 *When!* an impatient exclamation.
257 *credit* reputation.
267 *infelicity* unhappiness.

CARIOLA   Let me but speak with the Duke. I'll discover
  Treason to his person.
BOSOLA   Delays: throttle her.
EXECUTIONER   She bites: and scratches.
CARIOLA   If you kill me now
  I am damn'd. I have not been at confession   255
  This two years.
BOSOLA   When!
CARIOLA   I am quick with child.
BOSOLA   Why then,
  Your credit's sav'd: bear her into th' next room.
  Let this lie still.

(EXECUTIONERS *strangle* CARIOLA *and exeunt with her body. Enter*
FERDINAND.)

FERDINAND   Is she dead?
BOSOLA   She is what
  You'll'd have her. But here begin your pity,

(BOSOLA *draws the traverse and shows the children strangled.*)

  Alas, how have these offended?
FERDINAND   The death   260
  Of young wolves is never to be pitied.
BOSOLA   Fix your eye here.
FERDINAND   Constantly.
BOSOLA   Do you not weep?
  Other sins only speak; murther shrieks out:
  The element of water moistens the earth,
  But blood flies upwards, and bedews the heavens.   265
FERDINAND   Cover her face. Mine eyes dazzle: she died
    young.
BOSOLA   I think not so: her infelicity
  Seem'd to have years too many.
FERDINAND   She and I were twins:
  And should I die this instant, I had liv'd
  Her time to a minute.

271 **approv'd** confirmed.

280 **bad** instructed.

283 **meanness of her match** the fact that she married socially beneath her.

288 **gall** bitterness (see notes to Act 2, scene 3, lines 73–4 and Act 3, scene 2, line 154).

BOSOLA It seems she was born first: 270
You have bloodily approv'd the ancient truth,
That kindred commonly do worse agree
Than remote strangers.

FERDINAND Let me see her face again;
Why didst not thou pity her? What an excellent
Honest man might'st thou have been 275
If thou hadst borne her to some sanctuary!
Or, bold in a good cause, oppos'd thyself
With thy advanced sword above thy head,
Between her innocence and my revenge!
I bad thee, when I was distracted of my wits, 280
Go kill my dearest friend, and thou hast done't.
For let me but examine well the cause;
What was the meanness of her match to me?
Only I must confess, I had a hope,
Had she continu'd widow, to have gain'd 285
An infinite mass of treasure by her death:
And that was the main cause; her marriage,
That drew a stream of gall quite through my heart;
For thee, (as we observe in tragedies
That a good actor many times is curs'd 290
For playing a villain's part) I hate thee for't:
And, for my sake, say thou hast done much ill,
well.

BOSOLA Let me quicken your memory: for I perceive
You are falling into ingratitude. I challenge
The reward due to my service.

FERDINAND I'll tell thee, 295
What I'll give thee —

BOSOLA Do.

FERDINAND I'll give thee a pardon
For this murther.

BOSOLA Ha?

FERDINAND Yes: and 'tis

307 **perverted quite**   completely perverted, corrupted.

313 **pension**   i.e. payment for the murders.

316 **him which binds the devils**   God.

319 **worthy**   meant sarcastically.

322 **chain'd bullets**   chained cannon balls, used to wreck ships' rigging.

323–4 **for treason ... a blood**   treachery, like the plague, infects families.

The largest bounty I can study to do thee.
By what authority didst thou execute
This bloody sentence?
BOSOLA   By yours.
FERDINAND   Mine? Was I her judge?   300
Did any ceremonial form of law
Doom her to not-being? did a complete jury
Deliver her conviction up i'th' court?
Where shalt thou find this judgment register'd
Unless in hell? See: like a bloody fool   305
Th'hast forfeited thy life, and thou shalt die for't.
BOSOLA   The office of justice is perverted quite.
When one thief hangs another: who shall dare
To reveal this?
FERDINAND   Oh, I'll tell thee:
The wolf shall find her grave, and scrape it up;   310
Not to devour the corpse, but to discover
The horrid murther.
BOSOLA   You, not I, shall quake for't.
FERDINAND   Leave me.
BOSOLA   I will first receive my pension.
FERDINAND   You are a villain.
BOSOLA   When your ingratitude
Is judge, I am so—
FERDINAND   O horror!   315
That not the fear of him which binds the devils
Can prescribe man obedience.
Never look upon me more.
BOSOLA   Why fare thee well:
Your brother and yourself are worthy men;
You have a pair of hearts are hollow graves,   320
Rotten, and rotting others: and your vengeance,
Like two chain'd bullets, still goes arm in arm;
You may be brothers: for treason, like the plague,
Doth take much in a blood. I stand like one

335 **owl-light**   just after sunset, dusk.

337 **painted**   outward.

344 **sensible**   known through the senses.

346 **store**   restore.

347 **cordial drink**   medicine.

348 **opes**   opens.

354 **atonement**   reconciliation.

That long hath tane a sweet and golden dream.   325
I am angry with myself, now that I wake.
FERDINAND   Get thee into some unknown part o'th' world
That I may never see thee.
BOSOLA   Let me know
Wherefore I should be thus neglected? Sir,
I served your tyranny: and rather strove   330
To satisfy yourself, than all the world;
And though I loath'd the evil, yet I lov'd
You that did counsel it: and rather sought
To appear a true servant than an honest man.
FERDINAND   I'll go hunt the badger by owl-light: 335
'Tis a deed of darkness.

                                              Exit

BOSOLA   He's much distracted. Off my painted honour!
While with vain hopes our faculties we tire,
We seem to sweat in ice and freeze in fire;
What would I do, were this to do again?   340
I would not change my peace of conscience
For all the wealth of Europe. She stirs; here's life.
Return, fair soul, from darkness, and lead mine
Out of this sensible hell. She's warm, she breathes:
Upon thy pale lips I will melt my heart   345
To store them with fresh colour. Who's there?
Some cordial drink! Alas! I dare not call:
So pity would destroy pity: her eye opes,
And heaven in it seems to ope, that late was shut,
To take me up to mercy.
DUCHESS   Antonio!   350
BOSOLA Yes, Madam, he is living.
The dead bodies you saw were but feign'd statues;
He's reconcil'd to your brothers: the Pope hath wrought
The atonement.
DUCHESS   Mercy.

She dies.

355 **cords of life**   comparable to heart strings.

357 **turtles'**   turtle doves'.

360 **That**   it is our misfortune that . . .

364 **estate**   situation.

366 **fountains**   tears.

372 **dispose**   disposal.

375–6 **Where somewhat . . . dejection**   where I shall do something worthy of my downcast state of mind.

BOSOLA Oh, she's gone again: there the cords of life
    broke.   355
   Oh sacred innocence, that sweetly sleeps
   On turtles' feathers: whilst a guilty conscience
   Is a black register, wherein is writ
   All our good deeds and bad; a perspective
   That shows us hell. That we cannot be suffer'd   360
   To do good when we have a mind to it!
   This is manly sorrow:
   These tears, I am very certain, never grew
   In my mother's milk. My estate is sunk
   Below the degree of fear: where were   365
   These penitent fountains while she was living?
   Oh, they were frozen up: here is a sight
   As direful to my soul as is the sword
   Unto a wretch hath slain his father. Come,
   I'll bear thee hence,   370
   And execute thy last will; that's deliver
   Thy body to the reverend dispose
   Of some good women: that the cruel tyrant
   Shall not deny me. Then I'll post to Milan,
   Where somewhat I will speedily enact   375
   Worth my dejection.

                                   Exit (*carrying the body*)

2 ***Aragonian brethren***   Ferdinand and the Cardinal.

  misdoubt   doubt.

4 ***repair***   return.

6 ***cheat***   escheat – land held in escheat would revert to the previous owner if the holder died without heirs or was guilty of a major crime.

10 ***To be invested ... revenues***   to be given lands (and therefore income) which were Antonio's.

13–14 ***You are still ... myself***   you don't believe I can find a way of keeping safe.

18 ***suit***   request.

20 ***demesnes***   additional land.

Act Five

Scene one

(*Enter* ANTONIO *and* DELIO)

ANTONIO   What think you of my hope of reconcilement
To the Aragonian brethren?
DELIO   I misdoubt it
For though they have sent their letters of safe conduct
For your repair to Milan, they appear
But nets to entrap you. The Marquis of Pescara,   5
Under whom you hold certain land in cheat,
Much 'gainst his noble nature, hath been mov'd
To seize those lands, and some of his dependants
Are at this instant making it their suit
To be invested in your revenues.   10
I cannot think they mean well to your life,
That do deprive you of your means of life,
Your living.
ANTONIO   You are still an heretic
To any safety I can shape myself.
DELIO   Here comes the Marquis. I will make myself   15
Petitioner for some part of your land,
To know whither it is flying.
ANTONIO   I pray do.

(*Enter* PESCARA)

DELIO   Sir, I have a suit to you.
PESCARA   To me?
DELIO   An easy one:
There is the citadel of St. Bennet,
With some demenses, of late in the possession   20
Of Antonio Bologna; please you bestow them on me?
PESCARA   You are my friend. But this is such a suit
Nor fit for me to give, nor you to take.

34 **engag'd**   in your debt.

36–7 **How they ... ruin!**   how they make themselves strong through my downfall.

42 **ravish'd ... throat**   forcibly taken away.

43–5 **it were not fit ... my friend**   it isn't right that I should give something taken so unjustly to a friend.

DELIO No sir?

PESCARA   I will give you ample reason for't
  Soon, in private. Here's the Cardinal's mistress.   25

(*Enter* JULIA)

JULIA My Lord, I am grown your poor petitioner,
  And should be an ill beggar, had I not
  A great man's letter here, the Cardinal's
  To court you in my favour.

(*She gives him a letter which he reads.*)

PESCARA   He entreats for you
  The citadel of Saint Bennet, that belong'd   30
  To the banish'd Bologna.
JULIA   Yes.
PESCARA I could not have thought of a friend I could
  Rather pleasure with it: 'tis yours.
JULIA   Sir, I thank you:
  And he shall know how doubly I am engag'd
  Both in your gift, and speediness of giving,   35
  Which makes your grant the greater.

                                    Exit

ANTONIO (*aside*)   How they fortify
  Themselves with my ruin!
DELIO   Sir, I am
  Little bound to you.
PESCARA   Why?
DELIO Because you deni'd this suit to me, and gave't
  To such a creature.
PESCARA   Do you know what it was?   40
  It was Antonio's land: not forfeited
  By course of law; but ravish'd from his throat
  By the Cardinal's entreaty: it were not fit
  I should bestow so main a piece of wrong

179

49 **_ruddier_**   better.

57 **_apoplexy_**   see note to Act 4, scene 2, line 212.

58 **_frenzy_**   a kind of madness, 'inflammation of the brain'.

63 **_worst of malice_**   worst evil.

69 **_fraight_**   fraught.

72 **_infamous calling_**   ignoble life without means of support.

Upon my friend: 'tis a gratification   45
Only due to a strumpet; for it is injustice.
Shall I sprinkle the pure blood of innocents
To make those followers I call my friends
Look ruddier upon me? I am glad
This land, tane from the owner by such wrong,   50
Returns again unto so foul an use,
As salary for his lust. Learn, good Delio,
To ask noble things of me, and you shall find
I'll be a noble giver.
DELIO   You instruct me well.
ANTONIO (*aside*) Why, here's a man, now, would fright
   impudence   55
From sauciest beggars.
PESCARA   Prince Ferdinand's come to Milan
Sick, as they give out, of an apoplexy:
But some say 'tis a frenzy; I am going
To visit him.

Exit

ANTONIO   'Tis a noble old fellow.
DELIO   What course do you mean to take, Antonio?   60
ANTONIO   This night I mean to venture all my fortune,
   Which is no more than a poor ling'ring life,
   To the Cardinal's worst of malice. I have got
   Private access to his chamber: and intend
   To visit him, about the mid of night,   65
   As once his brother did our noble Duchess.
   It may be that the sudden apprehension
   Of danger (for I'll go in mine own shape)
   When he shall see it fraight with love and duty,
   May draw the poison out of him, and work   70
   A friendly reconcilement: if it fail,
   Yet it shall rid me of this infamous calling,
   For better fall once, than be ever falling.

74 **second**   support, as a second does in a duel, or the seconder of a proposal.

howe'er   in any event.

2 **instantly**   shortly.

5 **pestilent**   deadly.

6 **lycanthropia**   'wolf madness', see the doctor's explanation, lines 8–12.

DELIO   I'll second you in all danger: and, howe'er,
  My life keeps rank with yours.   75
ANTONIO   You are still my lov'd and best friend.

                                      Exeunt

Scene two

(*Enter* PESCARA *and* DOCTOR)

PESCARA   Now doctor, may I visit your patient?
DOCTOR   If't please your lordship: but he's instantly
  To take the air here in the gallery,
  By my direction.
PESCARA   Pray thee, what's his disease?
DOCTOR   A very pestilent disease, my lord,   5
  They call lycanthropia.
PESCARA   What's that?
  I need a dictionary to't.
DOCTOR   I'll tell you:
  In those that are possess'd with't there o'erflows
  Such melancholy humour, they imagine
  Themselves to be transformed into wolves.   10
  Steal forth to churchyards in the dead of night,
  And dig dead bodies up: as two nights since
  One met the Duke, 'bout midnight in a lane
  Behind St. Mark's church, with the leg of a man
  Upon his shoulder; and he howl'd fearfully: 15
  Said he was a wolf: only the difference
  Was, a wolf's skin was hairy on the outside,
  His on the inside: bad them take their swords,
  Rip up his flesh, and try: straight I was sent for,
  And having minister'd to him, found his Grace   20
  Very well recovered.
PESCARA   I am glad on't.
DOCTOR   Yet not without some fear
  Of a relapse: if he grow to his fit again

24 *nearer* more drastic.

25 *Paracelsus* Swiss medical authority, much revered.

26 *buffet* beat.

43 *way* an easy way.

51 *sheep-biter* a dog that worries sheep; a worthless cur.

I'll go a nearer way to work with him
Than ever Paracelsus dream'd of. If   25
They'll give me leave, I'll buffet his madness out of
   him.
Stand aside: he comes.

(*Enter* CARDINAL, FERDINAND, MALATESTE *and* BOSOLA, *who
remains in the background*)

FERDINAND   Leave me.
MALATESTE   Why doth your lordship love this solitariness?
FERDINAND   Eagles commonly fly alone. They are crows,   30
   daws, and starlings that flock together. Look, what's
   that follows me?
MALATESTE   Nothing, my lord.
FERDINAND   Yes.
MALATESTE   'Tis your shadow.   35
FERDINAND   Stay it; let it not haunt me.
MALATESTE   Impossible, if you move, and the sun shine.
FERDINAND   I will throttle it.

(*Throws himself upon his shadow*)

MALATESTE   Oh, my lord: you are angry with nothing.
FERDINAND   You are a fool. How is't possible I should   40
   catch my shadow unless I fall upon't? When I go to
   hell, I mean to carry a bribe: for look you, good gifts
   evermore make way for the worst persons.
PESCARA   Rise, good my lord.
FERDINAND   I am studying the art of patience.   45
PESCARA   'Tis a noble virtue; —
FERDINAND   To drive six snails before me, from this town
   to Moscow; neither use goad nor whip to them, but let
   them take their own time: (the patient'st man i'th' world
   match me for an experiment!) and I'll crawl after like a   50
   sheep-biter.
CARDINAL   Force him up. (*They get* FERDINAND *to his feet.*)

58 **Fil'd more civil**   trimmed more fashionably.

60 **salamander**   see note to Act 3, scene 3, line 48.

62 **cocatrice**   basilisk; see note to Act 3, scene 2, line 88.

   present   swift, immediate.

65 **brook**   permit.

70 **fetch a frisk**   dance.

75 **cullis**   soup or stew.

76–7 **anatomies ... Hall**   skeletons which he (the doctor) has put in the Surgeons' Hall.

FERDINAND   Use me well, you were best.
What I have done, I have done: I'll confess nothing.
DOCTOR   Now let me come to him. Are you mad, my
    lord?   55
Are you out of your princely wits?
FERDINAND   What's he?
PESCARA   Your doctor.
FERDINAND   Let me have his beard saw'd off, and his
    eyebrows
Fil'd more civil.
DOCTOR   I must do mad tricks with him,
For that's the only way on't. I have brought
Your Grace a salamander's skin, to keep you   60
From sun-burning.
FERDINAND   I have cruel sore eyes.
DOCTOR   The white of a cocatrice's egg is present
    remedy.
FERDINAND   Let it be a new-laid one, you were best.
Hide me from him. Physicians are like kings,
They brook no contradiction.
DOCTOR   Now he begins   65
To fear me; now let me alone with him.

(FERDINAND *tries to take off his gown;* CARDINAL *seizes him.*)

CARDINAL   How now, put off your gown?
DOCTOR   Let me have some forty urinals filled with
    rosewater: he and I'll go pelt one another with them;
    now he begins to fear me. Can you fetch a frisk, sir?   70
    (*aside to* CARDINAL) Let him go, let him go upon my
    peril. I find by his eye, he stands in awe of me: I'll
    make him as tame as a dormouse.

(CARDINAL *releases* FERDINAND)

FERDINAND   Can you fetch your frisks, sir! I will stamp
    him into a cullis; flay off his skin, to cover one of the   75
    anatomies, this rogue hath set i'th' cold yonder, in

79–80 **tongue and belly**   parts of the body left for the gods as a sacrifice.

90 **shape**   ghost.

104 **intelligence**   knowledge.

Barber-Chirurgeons' Hall. Hence, hence! you are all of
you like beasts for sacrifice, (*throws the* DOCTOR *down and
beats him*) there's nothing left of you, but tongue and
belly, flattery and lechery.   80

Exit

PESCARA   Doctor, he did not fear you throughly.
DOCTOR   True, I was somewhat too forward.
BOSOLA   (*aside*) Mercy upon me, what a fatal judgment
Hath fall'n upon this Ferdinand!
PESCARA   Knows your Grace
What accident hath brought unto the Prince   85
This strange distraction?
CARDINAL   (*aside*) I must feign somewhat. Thus they say
      it grew:
You have heard it rumour'd for these many years,
None of our family dies, but there is seen
The shape of an old woman, which is given   90
By tradition, to us, to have been murther'd
By her nephews, for her riches. Such a figure
One night, as the Prince sat up late at's book,
Appear'd to him; when crying out for help,
The gentlemen of's chamber found his Grace   95
All on a cold sweat, alter'd much in face
And language. Since which apparition
He hath grown worse and worse, and I much fear
He cannot live.
BOSOLA   Sir, I would speak with you.
PESCARA   We'll leave your Grace, 100
Wishing to the sick Prince, our noble lord,
All health of mind and body.
CARDINAL   You are most welcome.

(*Exeunt* PESCARA, MALATESTE *and* DOCTOR)

(*aside*) Are you come? So: this fellow must not know
By any means I had intelligence

106–7 **The full ... Ferdinand**   your employment in this business was wholly due to Ferdinand.

113 **I'll entreat**   I ask.

114–5 **Though he had ... would be**   if he were dead I'd help you gain what you desire.

117–8 **They that think ... begin**   if you think too much and ponder the outcome for too long, you'll achieve nothing (the opposite of 'Look before you leap').

124–5 **and style me thy advancement**   rely on me to promote you.

131 **school-name**   abstraction, i.e. does not take it seriously.

In our Duchess' death. For, though I counsell'd it,   105
The full of all th'engagement seem'd to grow
From Ferdinand. Now sir, how fares our sister?
I do not think but sorrow makes her look
Like to an oft-dy'd garment. She shall now
Taste comfort from me: why do you look so wildly?   110
Oh, the fortune of your master here, the Prince
Dejects you, but be you of happy comfort:
If you'll do one thing for me I'll entreat,
Though he had a cold tombstone o'er his bones,
I'll'd make you what you would be.

BOSOLA   Any thing: 115
Give it me in a breath, and let me fly to't:
They that think long, small expedition win,
For musing much o'th' end, cannot begin.

(*Enter* JULIA)

JULIA   Sir, will you come in to supper?
CARDINAL   I am busy, leave me.
JULIA   (*aside*) ·What an excellent shape hath that fellow!   120

                                                    Exit

CARDINAL   'Tis thus: Antonio lurks here in Milan;
Inquire him out, and kill him: while he lives
Our sister cannot marry, and I have thought
Of an excellent match for her: do this, and style me
Thy advancement.
BOSOLA   But by what means shall I find him out?   125
CARDINAL   There is a gentleman, call'd Delio
Here in the camp, that hath been long approv'd
His loyal friend. Set eye upon that fellow,
Follow him to mass; may be Antonio,
Although he do account religion   130
But a school-name, for fashion of the world,
May accompany him: or else go inquire out
Delio's confessor, and see if you can bribe

136 **_taking up_**   borrowing.

137 **_in want_**   needs money.

139 **_her_**   presumably the Duchess's – a long shot!

147 **_surer ... trace_**   better path to follow.

Him to reveal it: there are a thousand ways
A man might find to trace him: as, to know   135
What fellows haunt the Jews for taking up
Great sums of money, for sure he's in want;
Or else go to th' picture-makers, and learn
Who brought her picture lately: some of these
Happily may take—

BOSOLA   Well, I'll not freeze i'th' business,   140
I would see that wretched thing, Antonio,
Above all sights i'th' world.

CARDINAL   Do, and be happy.

Exit

BOSOLA   This fellow doth breed basilisks in's eyes,
He's nothing else but murder: yet he seems
Not to have notice of the Duchess' death.   145
'Tis his cunning: I must follow his example;
There cannot be a surer way to trace,
Than that of an old fox.

(*Enter* JULIA *with a pistol*)

JULIA   So, sir, you are well met.
BOSOLA   How now?
JULIA   Nay, the doors are fast enough.
Now sir, I will make you confess your treachery.   150
BOSOLA   Treachery?
JULIA   Yes, confess to me
Which of my women 'twas you hir'd, to put
Love-powder into my drink?
BOSOLA   Love-powder?
JULIA   Yes, when I was at Malfi;
Why should I fall in love with a such a face else?   155
I have already suffer'd for thee so much pain,
The only remedy to do me good
Is to kill my longing.

193

159 **kissing-comfits** sweets to freshen the mouth.

163 **Compare ... together** see yourself through my eyes.

166 **nice** delicate.

167 **troublesome familiar** tiresome spirit

170 **wants** lacks.

171 **I want compliment** do not know how to give compliments.

185 **scruple** scrap, tiny bit.

BOSOLA   Sure, your pistol holds
  Nothing but perfumes or kissing-comfits: excellent
    lady,
  You have a pretty way on't to discover   160
  Your longing. Come, come, I'll disarm you
  And arm you thus: (*embraces her*) yet this is wondrous
    strange.
JULIA   Compare thy form and my eyes together,
  You'll find my love no such great miracle.
  (*kisses him*) Now you'll say   165
  I am a wanton. This nice modesty in ladies
  Is but a troublesome familiar
  That haunts them.
BOSOLA   Know you me, I am a blunt soldier.
JULIA   The better:
  Sure, there wants fire where there are no lively sparks   170
  Of roughness.
BOSOLA   And I want compliment.
JULIA   Why, ignorance
  In courtship cannot make you do amiss,
  If you have a heart to do well.
BOSOLA   You are very fair.
JULIA   Nay, if you lay beauty to my charge,
  I must plead unguilty.
BOSOLA   Your bright eyes   175
  Carry a quiver of darts in them, sharper
  Than sunbeams.
JULIA   You will mar me with commendation.
  Put yourself to the charge of courting me,
  Whereas now I woo you.
BOSOLA   (*aside*) I have it, I will work upon this creature,   180
  Let us grow most amorously familiar.
  If the great Cardinal now should see me thus,
  Would he not count me a villain?
JULIA   No, he might count me a wanton,
  Not lay a scruple of offence on you: 185

188 **sudden** swift.

189–92 **use to ... together** are not restrained from our desires and won't put up with just wishing and longing.

200 **ground on't** cause of it.

209 **calling** profession.

213 **intelligence** information.

214 **cabinet** chamber, private room.

For if I see, and steal a diamond,
The fault is not i'th' stone, but in me the thief
That purloins it. I am sudden with you;
We that are great women of pleasure, use to cut off
These uncertain wishes and unquiet longings,   190
And in an instant join the sweet delight
And the pretty excuse together: had you been i'th'
     street,
Under my chamber window, even there
I should have courted you.

BOSOLA   Oh, you are an excellent lady.

JULIA Bid me do somewhat for you presently   195
To express I love you.

BOSOLA   I will, and if you love me,
Fail not to effect it.
The Cardinal is grown wondrous melancholy,
Demand the cause, let him not put you off
With feign'd excuse; discover the main ground on't.   200

JULIA Why would you know this?

BOSOLA   I have depended on him,
And I hear that he is fall'n in some disgrace
With the Emperor: if he be, like the mice
That forsake falling houses, I would shift
To other dependence.   205

JULIA You shall not need follow the wars:
I'll be your maintenance.

BOSOLA And I your loyal servant;
But I cannot leave my calling.

JULIA   Not leave an
Ungrateful general for the love of a sweet lady?   210
You are like some, cannot sleep in feather-beds,
But must have blocks for their pillows.

BOSOLA   Will you do this?

JULIA Cunningly.

BOSOLA   Tomorrow I'll expect th'intelligence.

JULIA Tomorrow? get you into my cabinet,

222 **Have conference with**   talk to.

223 **distraction**   madness.

225 **Yond's ... consumption**   there is my slow, debilitating disease.

230 **lead**   weight, as in the way secretaries and those privy to their employers' secrets took off lead seals from letters.

You shall have it with you: do not delay me,   215
No more than I do you. I am like one
That is condemn'd: I have my pardon promis'd,
But I would see it seal'd. Go, get you in,
You shall see me wind my tongue about his heart
Like a skein of silk.   220

(BOSOLA *withdraws behind the traverse; enter* CARDINAL)

CARDINAL   Where are you?

(*Enter* SERVANTS)

SERVANTS   Here.
CARDINAL   Let none upon your lives
    Have conference with the Prince Ferdinand,
    Unless I know it. (*aside*) In this distraction
    He may reveal the murther.

                                   (*Exeunt* SERVANTS)

    Yond's my ling'ring consumption: 225
    I am weary of her; and by any means
    Would be quit of—
JULIA   How now, my Lord?
    What ails you?
CARDINAL   Nothing.
JULIA   Oh, you are much alter'd:
    Come, I must be your secretary, and remove
    This lead from off your bosom; what's the matter?   230
CARDINAL   I may not tell you.
JULIA   Are you so far in love with sorrow,
    You cannot part with part of it? or think you
    I cannot love your Grace when you are sad,
    As well as merry? or do you suspect
    I, that have been a secret to your heart   235
    These many winters, cannot be the same
    Unto your tongue?

240 **_still_** continually.

242–3 **_if that ... know_** help me to help you by telling me.

243 **_judgment_** thought, sense.

257 **_breasts hooped ... adamant_** hearts strengthened with the toughest stone.

CARDINAL   Satisfy thy longing.
  The only way to make thee keep my counsel
  Is not to tell thee.
JULIA   Tell your echo this,
  Or flatterers, that, like echoes, still report   240
  What they hear, though most imperfect, and not me:
  For, if that you be true unto yourself,
  I'll know.
CARDINAL   Will you rack me?
JULIA   No, judgment shall
  Draw it from you. It is an equal fault,
  To tell one's secrets unto all, or none.   245
CARDINAL   The first argues folly.
JULIA   But the last tyranny.
CARDINAL   Very well; why, imagine I have committed
  Some secret deed which I desire the world
  May never hear of!
JULIA   Therefore may not I know it?
  You have conceal'd for me as great a sin   250
  As adultery. Sir, never was occasion
  For perfect trial of my constancy
  Till now. Sir, I beseech you.
CARDINAL   You'll repent it.
JULIA   Never.
CARDINAL   It hurries thee to ruin: I'll not tell thee.
  Be well advis'd, and think what danger 'tis   255
  To receive a prince's secrets: they that do,
  Had need have their breasts hoop'd with adamant
  To contain them. I pray thee yet be satisfi'd,
  Examine thine own frailty; 'tis more easy
  To tie knots, than unloose them: 'tis a secret   260
  That, like a ling'ring poison, may chance lie
  Spread in thy veins, and kill thee seven year hence.
JULIA   Now you dally with me.
CARDINAL   No more; thou shalt know it.
  By my appointment the great Duchess of Malfi

201

267 **how settles this?**   how are you taking this?
277 **hold**   stop.

And two of her young children, four nights since   265
Were strangled.
JULIA   Oh Heaven! Sir, what have you done?
CARDINAL   How now? how settles this? Think you your
   bosom
Will be a grave dark and obscure enough
For such a secret?
JULIA   You have undone yourself, sir.
CARDINAL   Why?
JULIA   It lies not in me to conceal it.
CARDINAL   No?   270
Come, I will swear you to't upon this book.
JULIA   Most religiously.
CARDINAL   Kiss it.

(*She kisses a Bible.*)

Now you shall never utter it; thy curiosity
Hath undone thee; thou'rt poison'd with that book.
Because I knew thou couldst not keep my counsel,   275
I have bound thee to't by death.

(*Enter* BOSOLA)

BOSOLA   For pity-sake, hold.
CARDINAL   Ha, Bosola?
JULIA   I forgive you.
This equal piece of justice you have done:
For I betray'd your counsel to that fellow;
He overheard it; that was the cause I said   280
It lay not in me to conceal it.
BOSOLA   Oh foolish woman,
Couldst not thou have poison'd him?
JULIA   'Tis weakness,
Too much to think what should have been done.
  I go,
I know not whither. (*dies*)
CARDINAL   Wherefore com'st thou hither?

287 *remember* recompense.

292 *lay fair ... Upon* try to disguise.

295–6 *go hide ... actors in't* get rid of those who did it.

297 *fortune* referring to his employing Bosola to kill Antonio.

300 *conduct* lead.

303 *the fire burns well* things are going well.

305 *smother* choking smoke.

306–7 *I shall ... churchyards* he has also carried the Duchess.

307 *grow* become

311 *their tails* the leeches' tails.

BOSOLA That I might find a great man, like yourself,   285
Not out of his wits, as the Lord Ferdinand,
To remember my service.
CARDINAL   I'll have thee hew'd in pieces.
BOSOLA Make not yourself such a promise of that life
Which is not yours to dispose of.
CARDINAL   Who plac'd thee here?
BOSOLA Her lust, as she intended.
CARDINAL   Very well;   290
Now you know me for your fellow murderer.
BOSOLA And wherefore should you lay fair marble
    colours
Upon your rotten purposes to me?
Unless you imitate some that do plot great treasons,
And when they have done, go hide themselves i'th'
    graves   295
Of those were actors in't.
CARDINAL No more: there is a fortune attends thee.
BOSOLA Shall I go sue to Fortune any longer?
'Tis the fool's pilgrimage.
CARDINAL   I have honours in store for thee.
BOSOLA There are a many ways that conduct to seeming   300
Honour, and some of them very dirty ones.
CARDINAL Throw to the devil
Thy melancholy; the fire burns well,
What need we keep a stirring of't, and make
A greater smother? Thou wilt kill Antonio?   305
BOSOLA Yes.
CARDINAL Take up that body.
BOSOLA   I think I shall
Shortly grow the common bier for churchyards!
CARDINAL I will allow thee some dozen of attendants,
To aid thee in the murther.
BOSOLA Oh, by no means: physicians that apply horse-   310
leeches to any rank swelling, use to cut off their tails,
that the blood may run through them the faster. Let

313 **train** accomplices.

313–4 **make ... a greater** take others with me.

316 **give out** let it be known.

325–7 **Oh poor Antonio ... dangerous** you need pity but to give it is dangerous.

329 **frost-nail'd** have the security of special nails in their soles.

330 **president** precedent.

331 **Bears up in** is steeped in.

332 **Security ... hell** lack of fear, as a result of which, they do evil.

336 **biters** blood-suckers; those who seek Antonio's blood.

341 **Haunts me** perhaps a ghostly vision is apparent here.

me have no train, when I go to shed blood, lest it make
me have a greater, when I ride to the gallows.
CARDINAL   Come to me after midnight, to help to remove
    that body   315
    To her own lodging. I'll give out she died o'th' plague;
    'Twill breed the less inquiry after her death.
BOSOLA   Where's Castruchio her husband?
CARDINAL   He's rode to Naples to take possession
    Of Antonio's citadel.   320
BOSOLA   Believe me, you have done a very happy turn.
CARDINAL   Fail not to come. There is the master-key
    Of our lodgings: and by that you may conceive
    What trust I plant in you.

                                                   Exit

BOSOLA   You shall find me ready.
    Oh poor Antonio, though nothing be so needful   325
    To thy estate, as pity, yet I find
    Nothing so dangerous. I must look to my footing;
    In such slippery ice-pavements men had need
    To be frost-nail'd well: they may break their necks else.
    The president's here afore me: how this man   330
    Bears up in blood! seems fearless! Why, 'tis well:
    Security some men call the suburbs of hell,
    Only a dead wall between. Well, good Antonio,
    I'll seek thee out; and all my care shall be
    To put thee into safety from the reach   335
    Of these most cruel biters, that have got
    Some of thy blood already. It may be,
    I'll join with thee in a most just revenge.
    The weakest arm is strong enough, that strikes
    With the sword of justice. Still methinks the Duchess   340
    Haunts me: there, there: 'tis nothing but my melancholy.
    O penitence, let me truly taste thy cup,
    That throws men down, only to raise them up.

                                                     Exit

6 **withal** also.
21 **deadly accent** gloomy, tomb-like sound.

Scene three

(Enter ANTONIO *and* DELIO; *there is an* ECHO *from the* DUCHESS' *grave)*

DELIO   Yond's the Cardinal's window. This fortification
  Grew from the ruins of an ancient abbey:
  And to yond side o'th' river lies a wall,
  Piece of a cloister, which in my opinion
  Gives the best echo that you ever heard;   5
  So hollow, and so dismal, and withal
  So plain in the distinction of our words,
  That many have suppos'd it is a spirit
  That answers.
ANTONIO   I do love these ancient ruins:
  We never tread upon them, but we set   10
  Our foot upon some reverend history,
  And questionless, here in this open court,
  Which now lies naked to the injuries
  Of stormy weather, some men lie interr'd
  Lov'd the church so well, and gave so largely to't,   15
  They thought it should have canopi'd their bones
  Till doomsday. But all things have their end:
  Churches and cities, which have diseases like to men
  Must have like death that we have.
ECHO   *Like death that we have.*
DELIO   Now the echo hath caught you.
ANTONIO   It groan'd, methought, and gave   20
  A very deadly accent!
ECHO   *Deadly accent.*
DELIO   I told you 'twas a pretty one. You may make it
  A huntsman, or a falconer, a musician
  Or a thing of sorrow.
ECHO   *A thing of sorrow.*
ANTONIO   Ay sure: that suits it best.
ECHO   *That suits it best.*   25

30 **moderate** reduce.

45 **ague** torment.

50 **second** see note to scene I, line 74.

51 **his own blood** the Cardinal's nephew.

ANTONIO 'Tis very like my wife's voice.

ECHO *Ay, wife's voice.*

DELIO Come: let's walk farther from't:
  I would not have you go to th' Cardinal's tonight:
  Do not.

ECHO *Do not.*

DELIO Wisdom doth not more moderate wasting sorrow 30
  Than time: take time for't: be mindful of thy safety.

ECHO *Be mindful of thy safety.*

ANTONIO Necessity compels me:
  Make scrutiny throughout the passages
  Of your own life; you'll find it impossible
  To fly your fate.

ECHO *O fly your fate.* 35

DELIO Hark: the dead stones seem to have pity on you
  And give you good counsel.

ANTONIO Echo, I will not talk with thee;
  For thou art a dead thing.

ECHO *Thou art a dead thing.*

ANTONIO My Duchess is asleep now.
  And her little ones, I hope sweetly: oh Heaven 40
  Shall I never see her more?

ECHO *Never see her more.*

ANTONIO I mark'd not one repetition of the Echo
  But that: and on the sudden, a clear light
  Presented me a face folded in sorrow.

DELIO Your fancy; merely.

ANTONIO Come: I'll be out of this ague; 45
  For to live thus, is not indeed to live:
  It is a mockery, and abuse of life.
  I will not henceforth save myself by halves;
  Lose all, or nothing.

DELIO Your own virtue save you.
  I'll fetch your eldest son; and second you: 50
  It may be that the sight of his own blood

54–6 ***Though in ... our own*** Fortune contributes to our misery which we can rise above if we suffer with dignity.

3 ***suffer*** allow.

5 ***distract*** inflame.

9 ***enjoin'd*** sworn.

10 ***sensibly*** feelingly.

17 ***protested against it*** promised not to.

Spread in so sweet a figure, may beget
The more compassion.

ANTONIO   However, fare you well.
Though in our miseries Fortune hath a part
Yet, in our noble sufferings, she hath none: 55
Contempt of pain, that we may call our own.

Exeunt

Scene four

(*Enter* CARDINAL, PESCARA, MALATESTE, RODERIGO, GRISOLAN)

CARDINAL You shall not watch tonight by the sick
    Prince;
His Grace is very well recover'd.
MALATESTE Good my lord, suffer us.
CARDINAL   Oh, by no means:
The noise and change of object in his eye
Doth more distract him. I pray, all to bed,   5
And though you hear him in his violent fit,
Do not rise, I entreat you.
PESCARA   So sir, we shall not —
CARDINAL Nay, I must have you promise
Upon your honours, for I was enjoin'd to't
By himself; and he seem'd to urge it sensibly.   10
PESCARA Let our honours bind this trifle.
CARDINAL Nor any of your followers.
PESCARA   Neither.
CARDINAL It may be to make trial of your promise
When he's asleep, myself will rise, and feign
Some of his mad tricks, and cry out for help,   15
And feign myself in danger.
MALATESTE   If your throat were cutting,
I'll'd not come at you, now I have protested against it.
CARDINAL Why, I thank you.

(*Withdraws*)

19 **osier** slender wands of willow.

32 **one's** someone's.

GRISOLAN   'Twas a foul storm tonight.

RODERIGO   The Lord Ferdinand's chamber shook like an
    osier.

MALATESTE   'Twas nothing but pure kindness in the
    devil,   20
    To rock his own child.

              Exeunt RODERIGO, MALATESTE, PESCARA, GRISOLAN

CARDINAL   The reason why I would not suffer these
    About my brother, is because at midnight
    I may with better privacy convey
    Julia's body to her own lodging. O, my conscience!   25
    I would pray now: but the devil takes away my heart
    For having any confidence in prayer.
    About this hour I appointed Bosola
    To fetch the body: when he hath serv'd my turn,
    He dies.   30

                                             Exit

(*Enter* BOSOLA)

BOSOLA   Ha! 'twas the Cardinal's voice. I heard him
    name
    Bosola, and my death: listen, I hear one's footing.

(*Enter* FERDINAND)

FERDINAND   Strangling is a very quiet death.

BOSOLA   Nay then I see, I must stand upon my guard.

FERDINAND   What say' to that? Whisper, softly: do you
    agree to't?   35
    So it must be done i'th' dark: the Cardinal
    Would not for a thousand pounds the doctor should
    see it.

                                             Exit

39 **desert**   just rewards.

   nor ... breath   and Christian beliefs are irrelevant.

42 *him*   the Cardinal.

46 *suit*   quest.

51 ***Smother thy pity***   quiet!

53 *banded*   bounced.

BOSOLA   My death is plotted; here's the consequence of
   murther.
We value not desert, nor Christian breath,
When we know black deeds must be cur'd with death.   40

(*Withdraws. Enter* ANTONIO *and a* SERVANT)

SERVANT   Here stay sir, and be confident, I pray:
   I'll fetch you a dark lanthorn.

                                                  Exit

ANTONIO   Could I take him
   At his prayers, there were hope of pardon.
BOSOLA   Fall right my sword: (*strikes* ANTONIO *down from*
   behind)
   I'll not give thee so much leisure as to pray.   45
ANTONIO   Oh, I am gone. Thou hast ended a long suit,
   In a minute.
BOSOLA   What art thou?
ANTONIO   A most wretched thing
   That only have thy benefit in death,
   To appear myself.

(*Enter* SERVANT *with a dark lanthorn*)

SERVANT   Where are you sir?
ANTONIO   Very near my home. Bosola?
SERVANT   Oh misfortune!   50
BOSOLA   (*to* SERVANT) Smother thy pity, thou art dead
   else. Antonio!
   The man I would have sav'd 'bove mine own life!
   We are merely the stars' tennis-balls, struck and
   banded
   Which way please them: oh good Antonio,
   I'll whisper one thing in thy dying ear,   55
   Shall make thy heart break quickly. Thy fair Duchess
   And two sweet children —

61 *in sadness*   in earnest, really.

64 *wanton*   thoughtless, carefree.

    whose ... care   who only think of their pleasures.

66–7 *good ... ague*   the brief respites between bouts of fever.

68 *vexation*   suffering.

69 *process*   reason, explanation for.

71 *fly*   flee from.

75 *tender*   value.

78 *in the forge*   on the anvil.

79 *misprision*   mistake.

82–3 *look thou ... bears't*   be as quiet as the body you carry.

ANTONIO   Their very names
  Kindle a little life in me.
BOSOLA   Are murder'd!
ANTONIO   Some men have wish's to die
  At the hearing of sad tidings: I am glad   60
  That I shall do't in sadness: I would not now
  Wish my wounds balm'd, nor heal'd: for I have no use
  To put my life to. In all our quest of greatness,
  Like wanton boys, whose pastime is their care,
  We follow after bubbles, blown in th'air.   65
  Pleasure of life, what is't? only the good hours
  Of an ague: merely a preparative to rest,
  To endure vexation. I do not ask
  The process of my death: only commend me
  To Delio.
BOSOLA   Break, heart!   70
ANTONIO   And let my son fly the courts of princes. (*dies*)
BOSOLA   Thou seem'st to have lov'd Antonio?
SERVANT   I brought him hither,
  To have reconcil'd him to the Cardinal.
BOSOLA   I do not ask thee that.
  Take him up, if thou tender thine own life,   75
  And bear him where the Lady Julia
  Was wont to lodge. Oh, my fate moves swift.
  I have this Cardinal in the forge already,
  Now I'll bring him to th' hammer. (O direful mis-
    prision!)
  I will not imitate things glorious,   80
  No more than base: I'll be mine own example.
  On, on: and look thou represent, for silence,
  The thing thou bear'st.

                              Exeunt

s.d. **with a book**   symbolic of deep thought or melancholy.

2 *He*   the writer.

material   real, actual.

8 *ghastly*   dreadful.

10 *lightens*   kindles.

13 *out of thy howling*   out of earshot.

16 *unseasonable*   too late, pointless.

17 *confin'd your flight*   cut off your escape route.

s.d. **above**   i.e. the gallery.

Scene five

(*Enter* CARDINAL *with a book*)

CARDINAL   I am puzzl'd in a question about hell:
He says, in hell there's one material fire,
And yet it shall not burn all men alike.
Lay him by. How tedious is a guilty conscience!
When I look into the fishponds, in my garden,   5
Methinks I see a thing arm'd with a rake
That seems to strike at me. Now? Art thou come?

(*Enter* BOSOLA *and* SERVANT *with* ANTONIO'S *body*)

Thou look'st ghastly:
There sits in thy face some great determination,
Mix'd with some fear.
BOSOLA   Thus it lightens into action: 10
I am come to kill thee.
CARDINAL   Ha? Help! our guard!
BOSOLA   Thou art deceiv'd:
They are out of thy howling.
CARDINAL   Hold: and I will faithfully divide
Revenues with thee.
BOSOLA   Thy prayers and proffers   15
Are both unseasonable.
CARDINAL   Raise the watch:
We are betray'd!
BOSOLA   I have confin'd your flight:
I'll suffer your retreat to Julia's chamber,
But no further.
CARDINAL   Help: we are betray'd!

(*Enter* PESCARA, MALATESTE, RODERIGO *and* GRISOLAN, *above*)

MALATESTE   Listen.
CARDINAL   My dukedom for rescue!
RODERIGO   Fie upon his counterfeiting.   20

221

25 **honour**   promise.

30 **engines**   tools.

31 **aloof**   apart, from a distance.

34 **'Cause**   so that.

38 **sudden**   swift.

39–40 **Thou tooks't ... sword**   the representation of Justice is usually with sword in one hand and scales ('balance') in the other.

MALATESTE   Why, 'tis not the Cardinal.

RODERIGO   Yes, yes, 'tis he:
But I'll see him hang'd, ere I'll go down to him.

CARDINAL   Here's a plot upon me; I am assaulted. I
am lost,
Unless some rescue!

GRISOLAN   He doth this pretty well:
But it will not serve to laugh me out of mine honour.   25

CARDINAL   The sword's at my throat!

RODERIGO   You would not bawl so loud then.

MALATESTE   Come, come: let's go to bed: he told us thus
much aforehand.

PESCARA   He wish'd you should not come at him: but
believ't,
The accent of the voice sounds not in jest.
I'll down to him, howsoever, and with engines   30
Force ope the doors.

                                                    Exit

RODERIGO   Let's follow him aloof,
And note how the Cardinal will laugh at him.

                                          Exeunt above

BOSOLA   There's for you first:
'Cause you shall not unbarricade the door
To let in rescue.   35

(*He kills the* SERVANT)

CARDINAL   What cause hast thou to pursue my life?

BOSOLA   Look there.

CARDINAL   Antonio!

BOSOLA   Slain by my hand unwittingly.
Pray, and be sudden: when thou kill'd'st thy sister,
Thou took'st from Justice her most equal balance,
And left her naught but her sword.

CARDINAL   O mercy!   40

42–3 **thou falls't ... thee**   you are bringing about your own collapse faster than events can cause it.

44 **leveret**   young hare, helpless thing.

46 **alarum**   battle

47 **vaunt-guard**   vanguard.

48 **honour of arms**   right to retain arms after defeat.

51 **adverse party**   enemy.

56–7 **Caesar died ... disgrace**   Caesar defeated Pompey in civil war only to be assassinated later while at the height of his power.

60 **barber**   i.e. acting as dentist.

BOSOLA   Now it seems thy greatness was only outward:
For thou fall'st faster of thyself than calamity
Can drive thee. I'll not waste longer time. There.

(*Stabs the* CARDINAL)

CARDINAL   Thou hast hurt me.
BOSOLA   Again.

(*Stabs him again*)

CARDINAL   Shall I die like a leveret
Without any resistance? Help, help, help!   45
I am slain.

(*Enter* FERDINAND)

FERDINAND   Th'alarum? give me a fresh horse.
Rally the vaunt-guard; or the day is lost.
Yield, yield! I give you the honour of arms,
Shake my sword over you, will you yield?
CARDINAL   Help me, I am your brother.
FERDINAND   The devil?   50
My brother fight upon the adverse party?

(*He wounds the* CARDINAL *and, in the scuffle, gives* BOSOLA *his death wound.*)

There flies your ransome.
CARDINAL   Oh Justice:
I suffer now for what hath former been
Sorrow is held the eldest child of sin.
FERDINAND   Now you're brave fellows. Caesar's fortune   55
was harder than Pompey's: Caesar died in the arms of
prosperity, Pompey at the feet of disgrace: you both
died in the field, the pain's nothing. Pain many times is
taken away with the apprehension of greater, as the
toothache with the sight of a barber that comes to pull   60
it out: there's philosophy for you.

225

65 ***broken-winded*** like an old decrepit horse.

67 ***vault credit*** do better than I deserve.

70 ***on't*** of it.

71 **we fall by** our downfall is caused by.

72 **Like ... diamonds dust** our own flaws are responsible for it.

74 ***I hold ... teeth*** my soul is about to pass from me.

84 ***main of all*** most of it.

BOSOLA Now my revenge is perfect: sink, thou main
   cause
  Of my undoing: the last part of my life
  Hath done me best service.

He kills FERDINAND.

FERDINAND Give me some wet hay, I am broken winded. 65
  I do account this world but a dog-kennel:
  I will vault credit, and affect high pleasures
  Beyond death.
BOSOLA He seems to come to himself,
  Now he's so near the bottom.
FERDINAND My sister, oh! my sister, there's the cause
  on't. 70
  Whether we fall by ambition, blood, or lust,
  Like diamonds we are cut with our own dust.

(Dies)

CARDINAL Thou hast thy payment too.
BOSOLA Yes, I hold my weary soul in my teeth;
  'Tis ready to part from me. I do glory 75
  That thou, which stood'st like a huge pyramid
  Begun upon a large and ample base,
  Shalt end in a little point, a kind of nothing.

(*Enter* PESCARA, MALATESTE, RODERIGO *and* GRISOLAN)

PESCARA How now, my lord?
MALATESTE O sad disaster!
RODERIGO How comes this?
BOSOLA Revenge, for the Duchess of Malfi, murdered 80
  By th'Aragonian brethren; for Antonio,
  Slain by this hand; for lustful Julia,
  Poison'd by this man; and lastly, for myself,
  That was an actor in the main of all
  Much 'gainst mine own good nature, yet i'th' end 85
  Neglected.

88 **i'th'rushes**   i.e. on the floor.

93 **In a mist**   in a haze, unclearly.

96 **dead walls**   as in walls that comprise a dead end.

99 **so good a quarrel**   i.e. taking Antonio's side.

102 **stagger**   waver.

109 **arm'd**   prepared.

112 **In's mother's right**   as his mother's heir.

   eminent things   the brothers.

PESCARA   How now, my lord?

CARDINAL   Look to my brother:
  He gave us these large wounds, as we were struggling
  Here i'th'rushes. And now, I pray, let me
  Be laid by, and never thought of.

(*Dies*)

PESCARA   How fatally, it seems, he did withstand   90
  His own rescue!

MALATESTE   Thou wretched thing of blood,
  How came Antonio by his death?

BOSOLA   In a mist: I know not how;
  Such a mistake as I have often seen
  In a play. Oh, I am gone: 95
  We are only like dead walls, or vaulted graves
  That, ruin'd, yields no echo. Fare you well;
  It may be pain: but no harm to me to die
  In so good a quarrel. Oh this gloomy world,
  In what a shadow, or deep pit of darkness   100
  Doth, womanish, and fearful, mankind live?
  Let worthy minds ne'er stagger in distrust
  To suffer death or shame for what is just:
  Mine is another voyage.

(*Dies*)

PESCARA   The noble Delio, as I came to th'palace,   105
  Told me of Antonio's being here, and show'd me
  A pretty gentleman his son and heir.

(*Enter* DELIO *with* ANTONIO'S *son*)

MALATESTE   O sir, you come too late.

DELIO   I heard so, and
  Was arm'd for't ere I came. Let us make noble use
  Of this great ruin; and join all our force   110
  To establish this young hopeful gentleman
  In's mother's right. These wretched eminent things

Leave no more fame behind 'em, than should one
Fall in a frost, and leave his print in snow,
As soon as the sun shines, it ever melts   115
Both form and matter. I have ever thought
Nature doth nothing so great for great men,
As when she's pleas'd to make them lords of truth:
Integrity of life is fame's best friend,
Which nobly, beyond death, shall crown the end.   120

Exeunt

Study programme

Reading the text

The following questions/tasks are intended to help you interpret the text as you encounter it. If answered in detail, they will provide you with much of the information you need to attempt the essay questions that follow. All can be used as the basis for discussion activities in seminar groups.

Act I

Scene 1

1. Read Antonio's speech describing the French court, lines 4–22. Why do you think this description, which is not essential to the plot, is included at the beginning of the play?

2. Read Antonio's description of Bosola, lines 23–28 and 75–78, and consider Bosola's behaviour in this scene. What feelings is Webster trying to create in the audience about this character?

Scene 2

3. What does Antonio's description of the Duchess, lines 112 to 129, show about his feelings for her?

4. Look at lines 148–155 and consider the exchange between Ferdinand and Bosola which follows. What is the nature of the relationship between Bosola and the two brothers?

5. What is the purpose of the Cardinal's and Ferdinand's words to the Duchess, from line 216? What is her reaction to their advice?

6 At what point in the conversation between the Duchess and Antonio do you realise that she asking him to marry her?

Act I summary questions

1 What are the three major events of the first Act?

2 What is your opinion of the character of the Duchess at this stage?

3 Is there any evidence for Bosola's low opinion of the brothers in the first Act?

Act 2

Scene 1

1 'I have other work on foot,' says Bosola in line 70. What is this work and how well does he do it during this scene?

Scene 2

2 What is the real reason that everyone should be confined to their rooms as Antonio announces in line 50?

Scene 3

3 How apt are Antonio's parting lines (51–2)?

Scene 4

4 Read the conversation between Julia and the Cardinal, lines 1–39. What does it add to your understanding of his character?

Scene 5

5 What answer could be made to the Cardinal's question in lines 16–17?

6 Put Ferdinand's threat (lines 78–80) into modern colloquial English.

Act 2 summary questions

1 What have you learned about Ferdinand and the Cardinal in this Act?

2 Which character makes the biggest impression in this Act?

3 What consequences might be predicted following from the action so far?

Act 3

Scene 1

1 Read lines 1–37. Sum up what has happened during Delio's absence, including the effects of events on the reputations of the Duchess and Antonio.

Scene 2

2 What impression do we get of domestic life in the first 61 lines of the scene?

3 What effect do Ferdinand's words have on the Duchess?

4 Explain the reasons for the Duchess's dismissal of Antonio from line 165. How does Bosola in turn deceive her?

Scene 3

5 In what ways has the Duchess made religion 'her riding hood/To keep her from the sun and tempest' (lines 59–60)?

Scene 5

6 Compare Bosola's opinions of Antonio in this scene with those he expresses in Act 3, scene 2.

7 Why do the Duchess and Antonio separate?

Act 3 summary questions

1 What is your opinion of Antonio's character at this stage in the play?

2 What are the major events of Act 3?

3 Does the atmosphere of Act 3 differ from that of the previous Acts?

Act 4

Scene 1

1 What tricks does Ferdinand play on the Duchess in this scene? What effect might these have on the audience?

2 What moods and emotions does the Duchess experience as this scene progresses?

Scene 2

3 Read lines 24 to 31. What does this speech show about the Duchess?

4 What do the madmen add to the scene?

5. How does Bosola's attitude to the Duchess change during this scene? What is his attitude to Ferdinand:

- immediately after the murders
- by the end of the scene?

6. Read Ferdinand's speech, lines 273–292. How far can we believe what he says?

Act 4 summary questions

1. Do either Bosola or the Duchess reveal new characteristics in this Act?

2. What evidence is there of Ferdinand's growing madness?

3. What aspects of the plot still need to be resolved?

Act 5

Scene 1

1. What does Delio ask of Pescara and why does he refuse?

2. Read Antonio's speech, lines 61–73, and explain his intentions.

Scene 2

3. Explain the Cardinal's aside in lines 103–107.

4. Why does Julia try to prise information from the Cardinal?

5. Read lines 333–343 and put them into modern English.

Scene 3

6 What does the echo scene contribute to the play?

Scene 4

7 Explain the confusion which leads to Antonio's death.

Scene 5

8 Read Bosola's speech lines 80–86. How accurate a summary is it of the events which it describes?

Act 5 summary question

What are the difficulties in staging Act 5? Can you see any ways of overcoming them?

Language

1 The play was originally dedicated to the Right Honourable George Harding and in the Dedication Webster refers to the play in terms of poetry: '… such poems as this …' are his words to describe the play.

Select three passages, of at least six lines each, from three separate scenes which seem to you to be closest to what you consider to be poetry. As a starting point, you may wish to select one of the many definitions of poetry to be found in dictionaries and literary reference books.

2 There is much use of imagery in **The Duchess of Malfi**. See how many references you can find to the following images:

- witchcraft or sorcery
- poison, unnatural death
- illness, decay
- animals.

In each case record who says them and the context. For example:

Animals

Speaker	Reference	Context
Antonio	engend'ring of toads (I.ii.84)	describing C's character
Bosola	the melancholy bird (the owl) (2.iii.7–9)	hearing a noise in the night
Doctor	wolf	

This might be done best as a group activity with one person in each group concentrating on an Act or scene. Use the data as the basis for writing one of the essays in Assignment 3 below on Webster's use of imagery. You will also find the information useful when writing about character.

3 Write an essay on one of the following:

- Webster uses imagery to give a negative and pessimistic view of the world. Is this view substantiated by a close reading of the text?

- What are the major themes of Webster's imagery and what do they reveal about his view of the world?

4 Who speaks the following lines, in what context and what does it reveal about them?

a) *I never gave pension but to flatterers,*
   Till I entertained thee: farewell,
   That friend a great man's ruin strongly checks,
   Who rails into his belief all his defects.

   Act 3, scene 1, lines 90–4

b) *How idly shows this rage! which carries you,*
   As men convey'd by witches, through the air
   On violent whirlwinds: this intemperate noise

> *Fitly resembles deaf men's shrill discourse,*
> *Who talk aloud, thinking all other men*
> *To have their imperfection.*
>
> Act 2, scene 5, lines 50–5

c) *All discord, without this circumference,*
   Is only to be pitied, and not fear'd.
   Yet, should they know it, time will easily
   Scatter the tempest.

   Act I, scene 2, lines 386–90

d)   *... a Prince's court*
   Is like a common fountain, whence should flow
   Pure silver-drops in general. But if't chance
   Some curs'd example poison't near the head,
   Death and diseases through the whole land spread.

   Act I, scene I, lines 11–15

e)   *In all our quest of greatness,*
   Like wanton boys, whose pastime is their care,
   We follow after bubbles, blown in th'air.
   Pleasure of life, what is't? only the good hours
   Of an ague ...

   Act 5, scene 4, lines 63–7

f) *You may discern the shape of loveliness*
   More perfect in her tears, than in her smiles;
   She will muse four hours together: and her silence,
   Methinks, expresseth more than if she spake.

   Act 4, scene I, lines 7–10

5 Choose short passages like the ones in Assignment 4 above which you think are significant because they reveal something about the speaker. Jot down your reasons for choosing them. Pool the quotations with others in the group and arrange them according to the character speaking and the Act.

See how full a picture is presented of each character and note

where either a character, a particular trait or a part of the play is over- or under-represented. Discuss whether this is due to chance or is revealing about the nature of the play.

6 Write out a random selection of sententiae (see 'The language of the play' on page xxiii for a reminder of what these are). Investigate how easy or difficult it is for a partner to apportion them to characters in the play. What conclusions can you draw about the contribution of sententiae to *The Duchess of Malfi*?

7 It has been said by some critics that the richness and power of Webster's language declines after Act 4. Can you find evidence to justify this criticism?

Character

1 Consider the following remarks by Bosola. At what point do they occur and what aspects of his character do they demonstrate?

> Could I be one of their flatt'ring panders, I would hang on their ears like a horse-leech, till I were full, and then drop off.
>
> Act 1, scene 1, lines 53–5

> Never in mine own shape;
> That's forfeited by my intelligence,
> And this last cruel lie: when you send me next,
> The business shall be comfort.
>
> Act 4, scene 1, lines 131–4

> I will not imitate things glorious,
> No more than base: I'll be mine own example.
>
> Act 5, scene 4, lines 80–1

Now do the same with these examples from the Duchess:

The misery of us, that are born great,
We are forc'd to woo, because none dare woo us:

Act 1, scene 2, lines 360–1

I account this world a tedious theatre,
For I do play a part in't 'gainst my will.

Act 4, scene 1, lines 83–4

I have got well by you: you have yielded me
A million of loss; I am like to inherit
The people's curses for your stewardship.

Act 3, scene 2, lines 183–5

Select two other speeches from Bosola and the Duchess which you think are significant and explain your choices.

2 Select three extracts from speeches by each of the following: Ferdinand, the Cardinal and Antonio, which demonstrate different aspects of their characters. In each case, make clear the trait which is shown by the extract.

3 What do the characters of Cariola, Castruchio, Julia and Delio add to the play? Are they necessary or could any of them be edited out of the text without significant loss?

Select two quotations from each of the four characters which are typical of them. Write a brief character sketch of each to accompany the quotes.

4 What would be lost if the Cardinal were to be omitted from the play?

5 What is your opinion of Bosola at the end of Act 1? How does it change by the end of Act 4? Does Act 5 add anything new?

6 What changes in emotion do Bosola and Ferdinand go through in the last two Acts? Whose character do you find the more convincing?

7. Bosola takes on the persona of the melancholic, the detached and cynical scholar and the professional spy. Who is the real Bosola?

8. Is the Duchess an active heroine or does she merely respond to events?

9. 'A good man out of his depth.' Is this an accurate description of Antonio?

10. Does Antonio have any of the characteristics you would expect of a hero?

11. Compare the characters of Ferdinand and the Cardinal giving special attention to the way they react to events.

12. 'The Cardinal, for all his power, rarely takes a prominent part in the action.' Discuss this view of the Cardinal.

13. What can you deduce from the first lines spoken by the following characters:

   - Antonio
   - Bosola
   - the Cardinal
   - Ferdinand?

Relationships

1. There are only two examples of marriage in the play: Julia's marriage to Castruchio and the Duchess's to Antonio. One is characterised by adultery and the other by deception and secrecy.

   There are also frequent associations of marriage with death or with imprisonment, such as 'The marriage night/ Is the entrance into some prison' (Act 1, scene 2, lines 246–7).

What view of marriage does the play portray overall?

2. 'The relationship between Antonio and the Duchess seems harmonious and truly affectionate. Far from infecting the relationship, the secrecy seems to have given it added zest. It is one of the few points of moral or emotional clarity in the play.'

Do you agree with this assessment?

3. What are the other significant relationships in the play? What is the basis of those relationships? Add to the examples below:

Delio – Antonio: friendship
Ferdinand – Cardinal: brothers and conspirators
Duchess – Cariola: mistress and servant

You may find some interesting gaps in your list. For example, can the relationship between the Duchess and the Cardinal be said to be significant? Who has the greatest number of significant relationships and who the fewest?

4. Imagine you are Delio, writing to a confidante abroad at the end of the first Act. Write a follow-up letter at the end of Act 2, scene 1.

5. Put yourself in the situation of Cariola

- before the Duchess's marriage
- immediately after the marriage
- after the birth of the first child.

Write the entries in her diary on those three occasions.

Echoes from Shakespeare

1. 'I am a man more sinned against than sinning,' says Lear in Shakespeare's *King Lear*. Might the Duchess say 'I am a woman more sinned against than sinning'?

2. 'One that loved not wisely, but too well' is Othello's statement about himself at the end of the play. Could this statement be used of anyone in *The Duchess of Malfi*?

3. 'Thou, Nature, art my goddess!' exclaims Edmund in *King Lear*. Could this be said appropriately by Bosola or the Duchess?

4. 'Things bad begun make strong themselves by ill,' says Macbeth prior to the murder of Banquo. Would this thought be appropriate to either Ferdinand, Bosola or the Cardinal?

5.
> Such an act
> That blurs the grace and blush of modesty;
> Calls virtue hypocrite; takes off the rose
> From the fair forehead of an innocent love,
> And sets a blister there; makes marriage vows
> As false as dicers' oaths.
>
> **Hamlet**, Act 3, scene 4, lines 47–52

(blister = brand; i.e. branded as a harlot)

These are Hamlet's words to his mother. Who might speak them (and with what motive) in *The Duchess of Malfi*?

Doom, gloom and madness

1. Who says the following? Do you think these statements (and others like them) reveal a deep world-weariness in Webster or are the sentiments merely expressing his characters' view of the world?

> *I do account this world but a dog-kennel.*
> *In what a shadow, or deep pit of darkness doth ... mankind live?*
> *Pleasure of life, what is't? only the good hours of an ague.*
> *I account this world a tedious theatre*

2. Is there anything optimistic in **The Duchess of Malfi**?

3. 'A claustrophobic world of moral confusion, lust, revenge and bloodshed.' Is this an apt summary of Webster's view of life as presented in the play?

4. 'It shows a fearful madness,' says Cariola about the Duchess's behaviour. Madness is an underlying theme throughout the play. Make a note of where madness is referred to or, in your opinion, occurs.

5. What reason might Webster have had for including so many references to both madness and illness?

6. You might like to compare the madness of someone like Ferdinand with that of Lear in **King Lear**. What different kinds of madness are portrayed in **The Duchess of Malfi**? Are any of them similar to that of Lear?

Appearance and reality

1. There are many obvious examples of the gap between appearance and reality: Bosola pretending to be a loyal servant of the Duchess, for example. Make a list of the major deceptions in the play. Do these decrease or increase as the play progresses?

2. Bosola, being a disillusioned cynic, sees through most deception. Are there any situations in which he is deceived? Who are the characters who are most deceived in the play? What is the

245

consequence of each deception – both for the deceiver and the deceived?

3 'The lie is the brick which builds up the wall of deception and false appearance.' How many of the characters lie? List the occurrences, using the following examples as a starting point:

Character	Occurrence	Lies to	Says
Cariola	4.ii.249	Bosola	she is betrothed
Duchess	I.ii.226	brothers	she will never marry
Bosola	3.v.41–2		

What conclusions can you draw from the information you have collected?

4 ***The Duchess of Malfi*** opens with a series of private exchanges rather than public speeches. In Act 1, scene 1 we have Antonio and Delio talking, followed by Bosola and the Cardinal and then Bosola speaking to Antonio and Delio. The scene ends with another conversation between Antonio and Delio. How typical is this of the play as a whole?

The distinction lies not in how many people are talking at any one time but in whether they wish their conversation to be overheard. Who has the majority of private speech? In what circumstances does public speech occur? How frequent are:

- asides to the audience
- conversations that are overheard?

In many tragedies there are important soliloquies (speeches delivered to the audience expressing the character's thoughts). How frequent are these in this play and who makes such speeches?

Compare ***The Duchess of Malfi*** with another tragedy such as

King Lear or *Macbeth*. Do you notice similar patterns of private and public speech? Make a comparison with a comedy such as *Twelfth Night* or *A Midsummer Night's Dream*.

Plot

1. Write a summary of the play in fewer than 200 words. Make notes in the margin of things you have had to omit. Compare your summary with others made by members of your group. Is it possible to agree on a common version? (A word processor would be ideal for this activity.)

2. This is the plot summary of *The Duchess of Malfi* in the *Longman Companion to English Literature*:

Set in Italy, the drama concerns the vengeance taken upon the young Duchess for marrying her steward Antonio, against the commands of her brothers, the Cardinal, and Ferdinand, Duke of Calabria, who is her twin. Ferdinand employs an impoverished malcontent soldier, Bosola, as his instrument for the mental torture of the Duchess, but Bosola has a character of his own and is filled with remorse. The Duchess is finally strangled, but Ferdinand goes mad with horror at his own deed and ends by killing Bosola who has already killed the Cardinal.

If you could add another fifty words to this summary, where would you add them and what would you say? Again, this activity would best be done after having typed and saved the passage on a word processor.

3. The *Oxford Companion to English Literature* summarises *The Duchess of Malfi* thus:

The Duchess, a high-spirited and high-minded widow, reveals her love for the honest Antonio, steward at her court, and secretly marries him, despite the warnings of her brother, Ferdinand, Duke of Calabria, and the Cardinal, and immediately after informing them that she has no intention of remarrying.

Their resistance appears to be induced by consideration for their high blood, and by, as Ferdinand later asserts, a desire to inherit her property; there is also a strong suggestion of Ferdinand's repressed incestuous desire for her. The brothers place in her employment as a spy the cynical ex-galley slave Bosola, who betrays her to them; she and Antonio fly and separate. She is captured and is subjected to fearful mental tortures, including the sight of the feigned corpse of her husband and the attendance of a group of madmen; finally she is strangled with two of her children and Cariola, her waiting woman. Retribution overtakes the murderers: Ferdinand goes mad, imagining himself a wolf; the Cardinal is killed by the now remorseful Bosola, and Bosola by Ferdinand. Bosola has already killed Antonio, mistaking him for the Cardinal.

What information does this summary contain which is omitted by the previous one? How important is the additional information? How does it compare with the additional material which you would have added to the first summary?

4. This is part of William Archer's synopsis of the play:

(The next scene is) the room in her palace in which the Duchess is imprisoned. Ferdinand, entering in the dark, pretends to be reconciled with her, and gives her, instead of his own hand, that of a dead man, leading her to believe that it is Antonio's. Then a curtain is drawn back and . . . are revealed waxen images representing the dead bodies of Antonio and their children. The Duchess does not suspect the trick . . . and makes no attempt to approach or touch the supposed corpses. . . . Then Ferdinand releases the mad-folk from the 'common hospital' and sets them 'to sing and dance and act their gambols' . . . They indulge in ribald ravings and then go off again as Bosola enters, disguised as an old man. He announces himself as a tomb-maker, introduces 'executioners, with a coffin, cords and a bell' and proceeds to speak 'the living person's dirge' in order to 'bring her by degrees to mortification'. Then the Duchess is strangled, her children are strangled, and her maid Cariola is strangled, all on the open stage. Ferdinand goes mad at the sight of this slaughter house, and Bosola, suddenly penitent, sets off for Milan to carry the news to Antonio. In the fifth Act at Milan, Julia, the Cardinal's mistress, is poisoned; Bosola kills Antonio, mistaking him

for the Cardinal; then he kills the Cardinal's servant, the Cardinal himself,
and Ferdinand, who by the way is still raving mad; and Ferdinand before he
dies, kills Bosola. Antonio's friend, Delio, and one of the children are left
alive.

from the **New Review** 1892

Archer's view of the play has been criticised as unduly negative.
Discuss whether this description is inaccurate. In what ways
might it be considered one-sided?

5. The motivation of characters gives the plot its energy. Without motive, there would be merely random action or none at
all.

List the motivation of the five major characters as seen in the
first Act and describe the immediate and long-term consequences. Use the following as a starting point:

Character	Motivation	Consequences	
		Immediate	Long-term
Bosola	wants payment for previous services from Cardinal	Cardinal arranges a place for him in Duchess's household	Duchess's secrets are revealed to brothers
Duchess	wants to marry Antonio		

Go on to incorporate the Cardinal, Ferdinand and Antonio in
your table.

It may be that some characters cause more difficulty in this
exercise than others. This can reveal interesting facets of the
play and its characterisation, so make a note of items which
you find hard to decide.

In performance

1. The play has been described as 'dark' and as 'claustrophobic'. A number of scenes are specifically set in darkness or at night. Most of the remainder could be set during the evening, after dark. Are there any scenes which would have to be set in daylight?

   How many mentions of walls and prisons are there? How does this affect the atmosphere of the play?

2. Which would be the most difficult scene to stage? Why? How would you overcome the difficulties?

3. Describe how you would furnish the stage for the following scenes:

   - Act 1, scene 1
   - Act 3, scene 2
   - Act 5, scene 2

   Use sketch plan views to make your arrangements clear. Include the number and position of exits.

4. Would **The Duchess of Malfi** be easier to film than to produce on stage? Would you introduce scenes/settings other than those described in the play? Would the play work as a horror film or is there too little suspense?

   Write a shooting script for a four to five page section of the play. Indicate character, type of camera shot, action, effects and dialogue. Don't attempt to be too complex.

   Look at this example from Act 2, scene 2, lines 77–80:

ORIGINAL TEXT

Enter Cariola with a child.

CARIOLA
Sir, you are the happy father of a son,
Your wife commends him to you.

ANTONIO
                            Blessed comfort!
For heaven' sake tend her well: I'll presently
Go set a figure for's nativity.

SHOOTING SCRIPT

	Close Up	Antonio, thoughtful	
Cariola			*Sir*
		Antonio turns.	
	Middle Shot	Cariola enters with baby.	
	Close Up	Cariola and baby moving slowly forward.	
Cariola			*You are the happy father of a son,*
	Middle Shot	She places baby in Antonio's arms.	
Cariola			*Your wife commends him to you.*
	Close Up	A's face looking down.	
Antonio			*Blessed comfort!*
	Close Up	Turning to Cariola.	
Antonio			*For heaven' sake tend her well:*

Some lines might be omitted or altered; others might be introduced. Use your imagination but try to make the atmosphere of the resulting film as close as possible to Webster's intention.

Three extracts for detailed study

▣ Look at Act 1, scene 2, lines 216–262.

- Examine lines 216–223. Compare Ferdinand's statements to the Duchess with those of the Cardinal.

- The Duchess speaks very little here. What do you make of what she does say?

- Given the Duchess's silence throughout most of this passage – although she is the subject of the conversation – what should her reactions be for the audience which observes her?

- Comment on the use of imagery in this extract.

- Explain the following:

    Hypocrisy is woven of a fine small thread,
    Subtler than Vulcan's engine:

    lines 236–7

    There is a kind of honey-dew that's deadly:

    line 231

    like the irregular crab,
    Which, though't goes backward, thinks that it goes right,
    Because it goes its own way:

    lines 242–4

    I would have you to give o'er these chargeable revels;
    A visor and a mask are whispering-rooms
    That were nev'r built for goodness:

    lines 255–7

- What does the passage reveal about the attitude of the brothers not just to their sister but to women in general?

- What premonitions do you notice in this extract?

2. Look at Act 3, scene 2, lines 1–57

- How would you describe the atmosphere of this scene?

- What does Cariola add to this scene? How different would it be without her?

- Give the gist of Antonio's speech, lines 24–32.

- Why do you think Webster has given the Duchess only 15 of the 57 lines in this extract?

- Describe the relationship of Antonio to
  - Cariola
  - the Duchess as demonstrated in this passage.

- What happens immediately after the end of this extract? How does the rest of the scene develop?

- Explain and comment on the following:

  > I hope in time 'twill grow into a custom,
  > That noblemen shall come with cap and knee,
  > To purchase a night's lodging of their wives.

  lines 4–6

  > 'Twas a motion
  > Were able to benight the apprehension
  > Of the severest counsellor of Europe.

  lines 40–2

  > I do wonder why hard favour'd ladies
  > For the most part, keep worse-favour'd waiting-women,
  > To attend them, and cannot endure fair ones.

  lines 45–7

3. Look at Act 4, scene 1, lines 29 (enter Ferdinand) to 90.

- Examine the language used by Ferdinand and make a detailed commentary on it.

- What do you think the Duchess means by 'a sacrament of the Church'?

- What is the Duchess's attitude to religion
  - earlier in the play
  - in Act 4?

- Why does Ferdinand twice resort to trickery in this passage?

- 'I will leave this ring with you.' What other references to rings does this echo?

- Explain the following:

> it wastes me more,
> Than were't my picture, fashion'd out of wax,
> Stuck with a magical needle, and then buried
> In some foul dunghill:

lines 62–65

> Portia, I'll new kindle thy coals again,
> And revive the rare and almost dead example
> Of a loving wife.

lines 72–4

> Good comfortable fellow
> Persuade a wretch that's broke upon the wheel
> To have all his bones new set: entreat him live,
> To be executed again.

lines 79–82

- What do you make of Bosola's three speeches, line 76 onward?

- What dramatic effects do you think Webster was trying to achieve in this extract? How far do you think he succeeds? How would you go about staging this extract for the best effect?

Study questions

1. To what extent is the Duchess to blame for her downfall?

2. Could it be argued that Bosola, not the Duchess, is the central figure of the play?

3. How far is **The Duchess of Malfi** a tragedy?

4. Is **The Duchess of Malfi** about power or about love?

5. 'Webster's view of the world is utterly bleak.' Use your knowledge of **The Duchess of Malfi** (and **The White Devil** if you have read it or seen it) to discuss this statement.

6. To what extent do the major characters develop during the play?

7. 'There goes no more brain power to the invention of these massacres and monstrosities than to carving a turnip lantern and sticking it on a pole' (William Archer, **New Review**, 1892). How far do you agree?

8. Is the purpose of **The Duchess of Malfi** to entertain or to educate?

9. 'The plot is far-fetched but the language is rich and evocative.' Is either statement justified? Would richness of language make up for an inadequate plot?

10. 'Not one of the characters is believable – but in such a play, this hardly matters.' How far do you agree?

Suggestions for further reading

Webster's other major play, **The White Devil**, is the most obvious complementary text. Tourner's **Revenger's Tragedy**, Kyd's **Spanish Tragedy** and Middleton's **The Changeling** are all revenge tragedies from the same period and could be usefully compared with Webster's plays. Indeed, any Jacobean play would be worth reading to gain a feeling for the atmosphere of the period.

It is almost essential to have read or seen at least one of Shakespeare's major tragedies such as **Hamlet**, **Othello** or **King Lear**. A biography of Elizabeth I, such as **Virgin Queen: A Personal History of Elizabeth I** by Christopher Hibbert, would not only give useful background, but provide an example of a strong female ruler who also had considerable difficulties with marriage. Any reputable history of late Elizabethan and Jacobean England would also be helpful, for example **Tudor England** by S. T. Bindoff. You could take this further by reading a study of Renaissance Italy, especially a history of the Borgia family. Try **Renaissance People** and **Renaissance Places**, both by Sarah Howath.

Wider reading assignments

1. What similarities and differences do you find, comparing **The Duchess of Malfi** with **The White Devil**?

2. Is **Hamlet** a revenge tragedy?

3. Compare Iago in **Othello** with Bosola in **The Duchess of Malfi**.

4. Is it possible to find a counterpart to the Duchess in Shakespeare's plays? Does she have anything in common with Gertrude (in **Hamlet**), Desdemona (in **Othello**) or Lady Macbeth?

5 From your reading of nineteenth-century novels, investigate the theme of love, marriage and the freedom to marry the person of one's choice. Is this a theme which disappears in twentieth-century fiction and drama?

6 How is the theme of revenge treated in contemporary fiction? Are there similarities to Jacobean attitudes to revenge and honour?

New Century Readers
Post-1914 Contemporary Fiction

Nina Bawden **Granny the Pag** 0 582 32847 0
      The Real Plato Jones 0 582 29254 9
Marjorie Darke **A Question of Courage** 0 582 25395 0
Berlie Doherty **Daughter of the Sea** 0 582 32845 4
      The Snake-stone 0 582 31764 9
Josephine Feeney **My Family and other Natural Disasters** 0 582 29262 X
Anne Fine **The Tulip Touch** 0 582 31941 2
      Flour Babies 0 582 29259 X
      A Pack of Liars 0 582 29257 3
      The Book of the Banshee 0 582 29258 1
      Madame Doubtfire 0 582 29261 1
      Step by Wicked Step 0 582 29251 4
      Goggle Eyes 0 582 29260 3
Lesley Howarth **Maphead** 0 582 29255 7
George Layton **A Northern Childhood** 0 582 25404 3
Joan Lingard **Lizzie's Leaving** 0 582 32846 2
      Night Fires 0 582 31967 6
Michelle Magorian **Goodnight Mister Tom** 0 582 31965 X
Beverley Naidoo **Journey to Jo'burg** 0 582 25402 7
Andrew Norriss **Aquila** 0 582 36419 1
Catherine Sefton **Along a Lonely Road** 0 582 29256 5
Robert Swindells **A Serpent's Tooth** 0 582 31966 8
      Follow a Shadow 0 582 31968 4
Robert Westall **Urn Burial** 0 582 31964 1

Post-1914 Poetry

edited by Celeste Flower **Poems 1** 0 582 25400 0
collected by John Agard **Poems in my Earphone** 0 582 22587 6

Post-1914 Plays

Ad de Bont **Mirad, a Boy from Bosnia** 0 582 24949 X
Anne Fine **Bill's New Frock** 0 582 09556 5
Nigel Hinton **Collision Course** 0 582 09555 7
Tony Robinson **Maid Marian and her Merry Men** 0 582 09554 9
Kaye Umansky **The Fwog Prince** 0 582 10156 5

Pre-1914

Charles Dickens **Oliver Twist** 0 582 28729 4
various writers **Twisters: stories from other centuries** 0 582 29253 0

Pearson Education Limited
Edinburgh Gate, Harlow,
Essex CM20 2JE, England
and Associated Companies throughout the world.

Editorial material © Addison Wesley Longman Limited 1996

This educational edition first published 1996
Fourth impression 2000

Editorial material set in 10/12 point Gill Sans
Printed in Singapore (KKP)

ISBN 0 582 28731 6

Cover illustration by Paul Hogarth
The Publisher's policy is to use paper manufactured from
sustainable forests.

Consultant: Geoff Barton

The text of the play is based on the New Mermaid edition
by E M Brennan, © Ernest Benn Limited 1964.
Published by A + C Black (Publishers) Ltd